FLOODWATERS

by Landis Lundquist

A story of Noah
and the building of the ark

Preface

Why Noah? Why now?

I'm convinced that the story of Noah is getting more compelling and relevant all the time.

If we say that this is only an old legend buried in antiquity, we may be missing its vital message.

Maybe, we should start thinking of it as a story for adults, not kids. It's not intended for coloring books or toy sets with cardboard cutouts and little plastic animals. This is an important historic account recorded in quite a bit of detail in the book of Genesis, about human violence, cataclysmic judgement, faith and salvation. It's much more than myth, or allegory. It was a turning point in human history recorded because it happened and is not to be ignored. If we could "flesh out" the story, put ourselves there in that tumultuous time, we may better understand our own times.

Just imagine how it might have been to face what Noah faced.

His family lived through the most shocking series of events. First, there was the message from God about the coming destruction of humanity, then the command to build a huge vessel far from the sea, then the great geological disaster, then a year cooped up in an ark with the entire animal kingdom. And then, an utterly new world!

They experienced, literally, the re-booting of life on earth. And, if the deluge did cover the entire earth as the Bible clearly says it did, then it could have reshaped the physical world, the sea and land, the rocks and gravel as the water receded. Many geologists are beginning to suspect that the gouged and twisted surface of the earth today with marine fossils on mountain tops and dinosaur bones heaped up in piles, can best be understood as the result of cataclysmic, hydraulic action, rather than slow erosion over eons of time.

I find these discoveries and theories of geology intriguing. We are constantly being asked to "trust science." But much of science is based on assumptions integral to a particular world view, one which I do not share. The world we walk around in today is not explained by a lot of current scientific theory. The Grand Canyon, for example, cannot be explained by slow erosion over eons of time. It is better explained as gouged out in days and weeks by vast amounts of water carrying gigantic boulders and mud. A flood maybe?

I find this scientifically disruptive thinking very fascinating and thought provoking. The theory of evolution, dependent on the magical element of eons of time plus chance, for me and anyone who stops to actually think logically, has never been a credible explanation of origins. If we go along with the crowd thinking of time as endless, that everything will continue the way it has always been, we could be buying into a flawed and dangerous assumption.

The reader can research creation science and history of origins. (There are hundreds of videos and books on the subject.)

This story is historical fiction. It is based on the biblical account, my understanding of current creation science, common sense and imagination. What *could* it have been like to be there with Noah? Extra-biblical names used in this story are common, ancient names from the Armenian Highland region of Mount Ararat.

This is my imaginary effort to put you, the reader, back in Noah's land, in the planning and building of the ark, with his three sons and their wives, there in Noah's walled property by the river, across the stone bridge from the violent city with its factions, corrupt officials and religions. I want you to hear Noah tell the great stories passed down to him from the days of Adam, Enoch and Methuselah. I want you to gaze up at the stars with Noah's family and wonder at the power and glory of this Creator God that Noah worships.

Landis Lundquist
Author

1

The Land

Back in time, not too long after Eve had passed away and Adam was nearing his end, a dove lifted off one of the lower branches of a tall, lone pine in the western hills, far inland from the sea, and glided out under a cloudless sky, exploring the landscape with her black, glassy eyes. As the morning mist lifted, she followed the downward contour of the land and was lifted by the warm morning air currents, as she sailed eastward out over the green plain. After some hours she came to a forested region which spanned the earth from north to south as far as her eye could see. Then, the forest gave way, gradually, to a plateau lined in long, surprisingly neat rows of fruit trees of various kinds. And then, beyond the orchards, were fields laid out in a kind of patch-work, through which ran a shining river, meandering east and west and disappearing into the haze where it met the horizon.

Following the stream, she saw in the distance columns of smoke rising from a sprawling, stone-walled city on the far side of the river with countless earthen structures and pathways where Man lived in large numbers. Just this side of the city, on the near side of the river, was a wooden-walled compound with its own set of buildings, connected to the city by a road which passed over a bridge.

Hovering over the compound she saw women hauling water in large earthen jars from a well, while others tended to sheep and cattle grazing in fenced-in pens. The outer wall enclosed a large space and was of woven willow branches, thick as a man's wrist and twice the height of a man.

As she descended, she saw a lone figure moving toward the back edge of the wall along a path that disappeared behind him into the woods. He was wearing a yellow tunic and a pale red cap.

She decided to rest from her journey there, on a branch. Without much interest, she watched this man move slowly along, arrive at the outer wall and enter one of its gates.

If she were not a dove, she may have quit watching this seemingly insignificant man and had the courage to fly over the wall of the city and spy on the people. There, in the haze of smoke, she would have seen ordinary things, skinny men pulling carts, merchants counting coins, women dying cloth in vats, stone workers chiseling, noisy children playing, dogs barking and beggars stretching out their palms. And she would have seen disturbing things: men cursing and wrestling in the street, prison gangs in chains and other things not meant for the eyes and ears of a dove. She would have not stayed long. It was just another smelly human, unpleasant place. Instead, she rested there by the walled structure on the near side of the river and watched the man in the pale red cap pass through the gate, greet a woman warmly and enter a dwelling.

9

That man was Noah. He seemed to be a rather simple man living in a rather humble place, but he was the most important man she would ever see. He was just returning from his morning walk and time of prayer.

The dove would not have been aware of the thoughts that troubled the man's mind or the violence and evil that pressed in on him and threatened to break him. She could not fathom the depth nor measure the weight of what he had just been shown. She knew nothing of what Noah now knew. She was just a curious, innocent dove. But she was looking at a man who had, moments earlier, just witnessed a troubling vision, and been assigned an immensely mysterious task by the God of Creation, the God he walked with and communed with every day on that path. Everything was about to change and he was the only one in the entire created world who knew it. Things were not going to continue on as everyone thought they would and insisted they should. The Creator God was going to intervene, and all would change, even her own world of birds and every living thing that had breath.

Noah, had removed his cap, and was sitting in his dwelling on a small three-legged stool, with his face in his hands thinking about how he could explain to his wife, his sons, and everyone what he had just seen and what lay ahead for them all.

2

The Times

The days of Noah were troubled days. They were days of progress without wisdom, days of gathering together without unity. The strong lacked mercy. The scales of justice were out of balance. Acts once thought treacherous and evil, were now celebrated. The most urgent matters brewing in the collective mind of society were the desire for self-gratification and the individual freedom to choose what is right and what is wrong.

From the time of Enoch, Noah's great grandfather, there had been a gradual, intentional retreat from the teachings of the forefathers who honored the God of Creation and submitted to his moral authority. It was said that too much emphasis had been placed on the old moralistic ways of the past, those old ideas from "the land of shadows." Why, the philosophical thinkers asked, should we continue to impose a system of rights and wrongs on everyone? Isn't it a bit arrogant to impose a certain Way, a one God or a singular Truth?

Ironically, replacing divine moral authority with individual rights led to the breakdown of society, the revealing of something dark and violent in the heart of Man and the domination by rulers who could enforce order and bring stability. This cycle of revolution, chaos, then tyranny and the loss of freedom, continued with each cycle growing in ferocity up until Noah's day.

Still, despite the growing insistence on freedom from moral authority, Noah pointed to the magnificence and startling beauty of creation and insisted that it continued to declare a design, an order, a transcendent power difficult to ignore.

During those days at the very beginning of this story, in the community across the river from Noah's property, town leaders had run out of solutions. The town elders there were supposed to provide direction and advice. But, though they had once honored the oral traditions of their own forefathers, they had adopted new ways of thinking and changed the rules to better please themselves. Decree after decree was written on stacks of clay tablets or stamped onto iron pillars along with legends and epic poems of larger-than-life men of valor. As the power of the rulers grew, true justice became more rare and defiance of the laws and rulers became more common and the reaction of rulers became more violent. The populace had developed a habit of defying authority and there were not enough civil guards and enforcers to keep order. The young, strong in body and quick to shout defiance, were always first to shake their fists in the face of authority and tradition, but, as in every generation, the young had just enough knowledge to be dangerous, and often lacked the wisdom needed to contribute to true progress.

There were also the opinions of the officials of the various religious sects in the district, each with their own pantheon of gods, their own temple and practices. But, thankfully, they kept to themselves, usually behind heavily latched doors. When they ventured out on the dirt paths of the city, they were hooded, silent and usually armed with a concealed dagger. There were often violent clashes between religious groups over ever redefined territories or doctrinal things few could understand.

Except for the sound of children playing here and there in vacant spaces, there was little sense of joy or wellbeing in those days in town or even along roads leading up to the walled city. Nearly everyone carried a stout walking stick and not just to fend off snakes or rabid dogs as in the old days. There was a sense of things unraveling. Everyone was on their guard against others. Systems of government that had brought a sense of security had become distrusted. Officials made promises but, in the end, it didn't seem to the people that their leaders could be relied upon. In the past, there were individuals esteemed by many for their moral strength and leadership ability. But in Noah's day, the intellectual and moral quality of both men and women had deteriorated. What had been taught by forefathers to be true and right was now considered judgmental, even hateful. Those who talked of God as *Lord* God having rightful authority had become the prey and had, in fact, been completely shunned from civic life.

Long before this time, in the days of Cain, people rapidly multiplied and had begun to congregate in large numbers for the sake of economics and safety. But humans proved to be ill-equipped to govern themselves successfully, all packed together inside city walls. There was a measure of safety in numbers from hostile tribes but, even with walled cities, there was never the feeling of complete security. The city near Noah's compound had held off attacks two or three times in recent years. But there was fear that enemy tribes were again building in strength. The walls and fortifications were well maintained and constantly being expanded. But, despite strong walls, townspeople were not safe from each other *inside* the walls.

Noah was well aware of all these issues.

The question of how society could unravel in this way was discussed often around the fire among members of Noah's family. They referred often to what they called, "Adam's choice." In their opinion, that's when it all started to go downhill for humanity. Eve made a choice, Adam followed along, innocence was lost. There was murder in the family. Cain killed Abel in a spirit of jealousy and violence had been festering and growing in the sons and daughters of mankind ever since.

Noah had told his family, "If you turn the ways of God inside out, you have the ways of mankind."

It was apparent to everyone, that humanity was groaning under the weight of self-inflicted pain.

For the people in the city, it was, "How do we survive the violence and deal with growing stress and anxiety."

For Noah and his family, it was, "How do we maintain a relationship with God in a corrupt and hostile world?"

3

The Ancestors

Noah's lineage is traced back to Seth, the third son of Adam and Eve. Noah's father, Lamech, was a young man, 56, when Adam died and he lived during the time of Enoch, another famous ancestor. Methuselah, Noah's grandfather, lived a couple centuries as a contemporary with Adam, so he knew Adam and Eve and likely sat many an evening listening to them tell all that they had experienced. And, very important to Noah's understanding of things, Methuselah lived during the time of Noah, right up to the year of the flood. So, all that was revealed to Adam had been passed on to Noah through Methuselah. Oral records were well kept, minds were sharp and men of old passed on what they had been told.

At first, it was an embarrassment to trace one's line back to Cain, Adam's first child, the murderer who fell "under a curse and was driven from the ground" and became a "restless wanderer on the earth." But as Cain's family multiplied and spread across the land, the story of Cain's treachery began to evolve into something to be admired. Strong, fearsome leaders emerged. Some gathered their followers into fortified places. They were the first builders of cities, the first workers of bronze and iron, the first to employ musical instruments and the first to practice polygamy.

Everyone on the planet knew about Adam and Eve and the story of beginnings. They had a vague notion of what sin was and there was a universal sense that they stood guilty before a righteous Creator God. It was readily apparent that the first couple's sin of disobedience and rebellion was still festering in the heart of humanity. But pride kept most from acknowledging any personal obligation or responsibility. When they looked around themselves at creation, they could see the vivid contrast between the power and magnanimity of the Creator and their own petty self-centeredness. Deep down, they knew they had fallen far short of what he had created them to be. But, rather than turn back to the Creator, people deceived themselves into thinking they could achieve a sense of righteousness on their own. They let their vain imaginations roam. There seemed to be no end to the creativity of mankind to invent ways of relieving themselves of the nagging sense of not measuring up. They devised an endless array of religious practices, sacrifice to idols, penance, self-denial, ritual, chanting, meditation, worship of nature, worship of knowledge and doing good works. And when these failed, they indulged in sensual pleasure. This led to perversion, human sacrifice and violence. It was all an attempt to fill the void of what was missing.

But Eve then bore their third son, Seth. It was during Seth's life that people began to remember their Creator and, as Noah's forefathers said, "At that time men began to call on the name of the Lord." So, Seth's line had a heritage of seeking out the Creator and desired to renew the relationship that had been lost. Both Methuselah and Lamech were seeped in this tradition and were alive when the three boys were born to Noah. So, all members of Noah's family had ample opportunities to learn directly from these forefathers who lived long, eventful lives. Scoffers called their beliefs archaic nonsense, "from the land of shadows." Nevertheless, these men, though not without flaws and failings, desired to have an understanding of the nature and workings of the Creator based on an oral history kept carefully in mind and heart.

They taught that humans were not animals, but God had breathed into Man a very special, uncreated life. Their tradition was that God not only revealed himself generally through creation, but that he could be known personally and, though mysterious, was not altogether silent. But this point of view was abandoned by all but a very few.

4

Noah's Sons

Japheth was the oldest of the three, then Shem and Ham. From birth he had shown himself to be practical, skilled with tools, able to take on tasks, to plan and execute. And he had the very important ability to lead others. He was able to solve problems, not only in practical things but in relationships with men older than himself, such as city officials. But, his self-confidence sometimes became over-inflated resulting in impatience with others. Noah looked to him for leadership in maintaining the compound and carrying out tasks at hand, but he often had to deal with Japheth's prideful attitude.

Shem was inquisitive and gentle spirited. He worked hard to grasp grand concepts and was the first to comprehend the over-whelming complexity of the vision of his father. He was the most like Noah in his life of the spirit within. He longed for that intimacy with the divine that his father often talked to him about. Shem, occasionally, accompanied Noah on his morning walks where they spent nearly as much time talking to the Creator God as they did about this Creator who had made all things. Shem was determined to understand all he could of the nature of God, his heart and his power to intervene in the affairs of mankind. It was an intellectual pursuit, a careful study, a systematic effort to understand the world and its maker, as well as a spiritual quest, a desire for relationship. It was Shem who asked about Adam, what he had known, what he had said. It was Shem, mainly, who passed this knowledge on to the next generation. Everything Noah told him, he remembered. And the wisdom he passed on became like the root system of a great, everlasting tree of life.

Ham was the kind of rugged man a person wants as a companion in a time of trouble or difficulty. He had a fire in his belly and had the physical size and strength to back it up. He was intimidated by no one. More than once he had returned home carrying weapons he had taken from the hands of those who had threatened him. And, he could work. He had spent his younger years working in Noah's forgery, combining tin and copper and drawing useful objects of bronze from the fire and beating them into useful things with a heavy hammer and forging objects in sand molds. He would sweat and hammer, pump the bellows and sing. Ham found joy in hard work and his attitude was contagious.

5

Noah, Man of the Soil

It was apparent by the size of Noah's walled compound and its commanding position on a major river, that he had achieved some success in his long life, despite living among a people, who, for the most part, shunned him for his unpopular beliefs. There was widespread respect for his ability to work the soil and produce goods which merchants of his day valued. Townsfolk's mouths were full of ridicule, but their stomachs were full of the fruit of his labors. A good portion of the market place displayed fruits, grains, herbs and root vegetables grown on Noah's lands and developed through his ingenuity. People envied his seeming innate ability to grow things, to understand the mysterious cycles of green plants, his insight into the strange death and resurrection of seeds and his success in drawing abundance from soil, which for them, yielded mostly blight and hardship. Noah worked the lands east of the hill country, a gradually sloping terrain of rich alluvial soil through which ran a system of clear, meandering streams.

He was a man of the soil.

He was not a rugged man, but early in life he had been sent by his father, Lamech, to learn the ways of the mining tribes of the north and had returned with useful knowledge in the making and use of basic tools. And, he was no stranger to hard physical work. He had trekked the forested regions of the east and had lived for more than a century among the peoples of the delta where rivers entered the sea. During these years he learned just how stubborn the earth was. But he wasn't one to give up on a task and, though people wanted nothing to do with his beliefs, they had to admit he got things done.

Noah became increasingly convinced of the validity of the tradition that there was a curse upon the earth as a result of the rebellion in the hearts of all men, including his own. He grew ever more confident that the words of his father, Lamech, were true, that a wisdom, acquired only through words of the Creator God and an understanding of his ways, was necessary for any hope of reaping a satisfying existence. His father spoke of this often. He called it "walking with God." Lamech had learned it from Methuselah, Methuselah from Enoch, and Enoch directly from Adam, the first man.

This tradition, this "walking," was just words repeated, stories whispered, promises remembered, warnings given, truths set to rhyming song. But it became a way of life. Blessings and curses. It all rang true to Noah. He could see it and grasp it. It all centered on what had been revealed of the unchanging nature of the Creator God. It seemed living and active. The longer he lived, the more it became the fixed star in his universe. And he was obsessed by its vital importance. It was the floating log onto which he clung in the raging river of his life. Except for rare moments of weakness, Noah's acts and thoughts were governed by his knowledge of the God he worshipped. He, and he alone, submitted his life to God's sovereign rule.

Noah strongly believed that the God who created the heavens and the earth was a living spirit, a personal God. It was possible, he believed, to "walk" in a kind of fellowship with this God as Adam and Eve did in the beginning. Yes, paradise was lost, mankind had fallen into depravity, but God hadn't changed. He was still the all-powerful, all-knowing, merciful and compassionate God of creation. He still desired to know and be known. His purposes in creating men and women as stewards of the earth hadn't changed.

In Noah's day it became dangerous to speak of the God of Adam and Eve, to mention how Enoch walked with his God and didn't die, but was "taken away." The God that demanded obedience was despised and rejected. New gods ran things now, more manageable gods, gods of stone and fire, gods whose bronze image you could carry in your pocket. It was a time of freedom to choose.

Noah chose to serve the God of his forefathers. Every other human chose otherwise. So, Noah, this man of the soil, this man of God, was an unusual man of his day and he had been given a task of the most unusual nature.

6

Noah's Walk

Shem had always been an early riser, getting up earlier than most others in the compound, because he had been responsible for getting the cattle fed and making sure the servants got up and were getting to work. Of all his tasks, these morning chores were the most enjoyable, to be out in the quiet of the day when it was cool. In those days, before the flood, especially during those months before harvest time, the bright sun quickly made everything hot. Mornings were to be put to good use.

Very often, back in those days, before Shem reached the cattle pen, he'd see his father's white and yellow tunic and pale red cap moving through the brush down among the trees near the meadow. There was a well-worn footpath from the gate of his dwelling, across the pasture, skirting the wetlands of the meadow and into the woods beyond. People had said that Noah walked with God and Shem knew better than anyone what that meant. He had been with his father down there on the path literally *walking and talking* with someone unseen.

He stood leaning against the cattle fence and watched him stroll along, his lips moving, his hands sometimes making gestures as if to an invisible companion. Even in the cold season, wearing his woolen cap and the shawl his wife knit for him, he would walk along, always down toward the meadow, disappearing into the woods, chatting all the way.

Many years later, Shem would understand better how those walks saved them all. They had been warned by God of things no one else had the ability to comprehend, or made the effort to understand. Noah sought out the counsel of God, took it to heart and, most importantly, acted on it. This meant much to Shem as he recollected events of that time. He attempted in his own way to imitate his father and have the same devotion to God, but he found it very difficult.

One day Shem and his brothers were called together to witness his father build an altar of stones. He took a small lamb, one that was pick of the flock and sacrificed it on the altar. It was not easy to watch. Noah was moved. The three sons stood and soberly observed their father kill, prepare and offer the lamb.

They couldn't help but wonder. They knew Noah had some rare ability to sense the very heart of God and know, somehow, what was to be done or said. The whole business of offering sacrifices of various sorts was a mysterious tradition. Each male child in their ancestral line going back to Seth, was instructed in such things and details of tradition were passed on. Sons of Cain, as far as Shem knew, had abandoned most of these sacred traditions and had adopted new ones. But one thing that seemed universally certain, was that everyone served one god or another and had some sort of ritual or practice that appeased those gods. Everyone was working at some form of salvation from the presence of evil in the world.

Shem, knew as he watched his father before the altar, that he had been born with a special purpose, born to a special family, born with a unique opportunity to see things most people would never see. His father, Noah, could look at a tiny cloud in the distance and know that rain was coming. If God had told him something, he took it to heart and it made him strong, stronger than any other man among the many people of the land.

It was apparent to the family that the hand of God was upon Noah, and Shem, especially, longed for the same faith he had, but, as most others, he was usually held back by doubts and fears.

"Believe big," Noah told him.

"You cannot measure what God can do," he said. "Take your cubit stick. Throw it away. It cannot measure what God can do."

Shem would always remember these pithy, prophetic words Noah often spoke.

On another day Shem caught his father returning from his morning walk and asked him, "Why do you walk when you worship and pray?"

His father answered with a wink and a smile, "So I don't fall asleep."

"Well, what's it like to hear God's voice?"

"Sometimes you sense God is speaking to you. So, you lean in, you try to be quiet and hear. You wait. His voice is never like a clap of thunder, but more like a whisper in your spirit. So, you think on it. You have a decision to make. Doubts come. But somehow you know. It gets into your heart and you know. And nothing can shake it loose."

Noah told him how he agonized over some things God had shown him. Is this really God's will?

Shem asked, "How can you afford to spend so much time every morning walking and praying?"

"Shem, you know how busy I am?"

"Yes."

"You know how much I have to do each day and how many pressing responsibilities I have?"

"Ah, yes."

"Well, how could I afford to spend *less* than an hour each day with God?"

After a moment to let the irony sink in, they both laughed and went off to work.

Noah had been through a lot in his long life and had acquired a storehouse of wisdom. Sadly, Shem was probably the only person he could freely talk to about many things. Shem's ears were open when Noah spoke and he gathered up his father's wisdom and stored it away safely.

7

Noah's Compound

As Noah's sons grew and found wives, they built their own dwellings in Noah's compound and helped to construct a very stout surrounding wall made of interwoven willow branches, a number of formidable gates of cedar wood thicker than the span of a man's hand, hinged by iron made in the family's charcoal-fired foundry, latched by a rough-cut oaken beam that slid into place on iron straps. To the side of the main gate facing the town was a small cove, four paces deep and six paces wide, formed into the wall where Noah received vendors, officials, inquirers. It was the place where agreements were made, disputes settled. This place was a "safe place" enforced by Noah's servants and honored by most townspeople.

Inside the wall, the sons, with the help of servants, built a covered walkway connecting the main, domestic buildings. There was a foundry, a water well house and a tool house, which was the large building on the north end where tools were stored and all sorts of projects were performed by artisans and hired craftsmen. Japheth spent most of his time in the tool house meeting with managers and overseeing work assigned by Noah.

Map of Noah's Compound

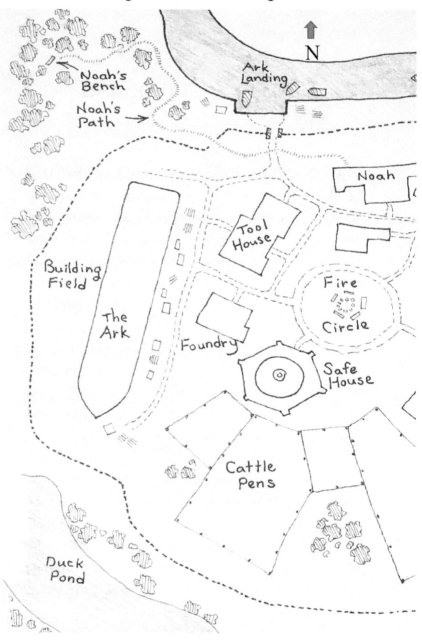

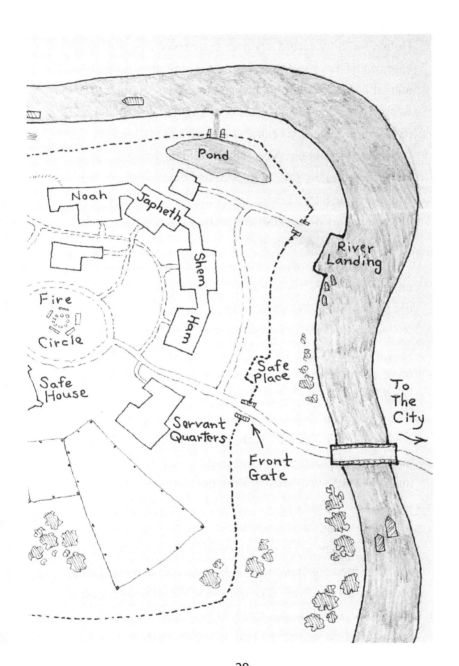

Pond

Noah

Japheth

Shem

Ham

Fire
Circle

Safe
House

Servant
Quarters

Safe
Place

Front
Gate

River
Landing

To
The
City

29

On the southwest side of the circular shaped compound, opposite the river, was what everyone called the "Safe House," a stout, secure structure that served as a fortress in case of attack, as well as housing for servants with its own animal corral, outdoor kitchen and tool shed. Similar to the larger compound, it was somewhat circular shaped and had its own secure door, a central courtyard and fire circle.

There was another very stout building of stone which safely stored grain, salt, cattle feed and food supplies. There was a covered pit for lime, a very valuable commodity which was made into white wash for coating interior walls and to sanitize the human waste pit.

The compound was located on a large flat piece of ground on the inside curve of a major river which meandered from the distant hills. Somewhere up in the high-country water welled up from the deep feeding the river. Only Noah had ever traveled to that distant place. It's useless to speak the name of the river here, since nothing remains of that place, not the river, not the hills, not the compound, nothing.

Several cart trails ran from the main gate into the compound to its various buildings, to the gate at the river landing and to each part of the property. One ran the entire inside perimeter and another from the tool house to the field where the ark was built.

One landing, at a sandy beach on the river bank, was primarily used by women and servants for domestic purposes and launching small craft for fishing and coming and going up and down the river. The other was cut more into a high river bank and was a more working landing reinforced against river current action with oak logs, ropes and devices for mooring river craft. A large oaken beam and fulcrum swung over the river for unloading barges carrying timber, mountain stones, lime stone, gravel and other heavy supplies needed to build and maintain the compound. Goods were coming from suppliers up and down stream that used oxen to tow barge traffic, especially during summer season when water levels were low.

There was a man-made pond fed by a stone culvert under the wall, which was a source of local water for households, for washing and a place for kids to fish and swim when the river currents ran too swiftly to be safe.

There was also a number of stables for oxen, mules, goats and pigs and a large sheepfold. Poultry, peacocks and pigeons wandered the empty spaces picking at bugs and making a racket.

The family lived in the main house, a high structure of straw-strengthened clay with a foundation of stone high as a man's shoulder. It had a pole and beam roof covered with shingles of split cedar. The main house had an opening in the center with a fire pit. Large hot stones were warmed in the pit and brought inside for warmth on cool nights.

Beds were four-legged wooden frames with intricately woven twine sleeping surfaces. Artisans would weave a unique pattern for each person.

The three sons lived with their wives in separate dwellings attached to the main house.

Outside the main gate, a road led a short distance to a bridge of stone and large beams which spanned the river and led directly to the western gate of the city. The city was ruled by three lords who competed for control. Smoke from a thousand fires drifted from the city over the compound night and day. The atmosphere was often punctuated, especially at night, by screams and the roar of large crowds. Men and women of the city came often to Noah's gate to the "safe place" for treatment of wounds. They came bloody and beaten to Noah's gate for protection and care. Shem spent a good part of his time each evening counseling distraught guests and sorting out disputes. The violence of the city and the surrounding lands was spilling over into Noah's life in the compound.

8

The City

A cross the river from Noah's compound was a city with hundreds of narrow lanes and pathways which wound throughout the place in no particular pattern. The main dirt roads all terminated at the center of town in a circular, sheltered market place protected from the sun and elements by a sagging roof of clay tiles held up in the center by a massive stone and earthen structure from which rose a continual cloud of smoke smelling of roasted grain. The outer edge of the market roof faced outward to the wide, circular street and was held up by wooden pillars dividing the space into equal sections. Venders occupying each stall displayed a myriad of dry goods, grains, spices, scented oils, fruits, fish, tools, daggers, jewels, idols, pine pitch, ram's horns, iron ingots, raw hemp, bundles of wool, woven cloth, animal hides and much more.

The sweet smell of roasted grains and foods prepared over open fires was quickly lost on the senses, for humanity passed, ankle deep in filth and mire along with steaming, plodding beasts of burden, hollering merchantmen, rattling ox carts, sellers hawking their goods, boys hollering, thieves, idlers and swindlers watching from the edge of the crowd. Clever tricksters were anxious to offer unsuspecting travelers services which may or may not include a cracked skull and an empty purse. Mingled together, the sounds of this throng, the bleating, barking, screaming, hollering and rattling raised a discordant din that echoed across the town lessening only as merchants returned home before the sun disappeared slowly behind the distant hills to the west when it was dangerous to be out alone.

Away from the market the lanes were filled with groups of women dressed in colorful, flowing cloth carrying baskets or jars, always wary of lurking men. Old men with walking sticks moved along awkwardly. Thin, boney men bent low straining against hempen shoulder harnesses, pulled heavily loaded, wooden carts. Naked children darted in and out among the wheels and donkeys driven along by cursing handlers delivering loads of vegetables, animal hides, kindling, sheaves of cut grain stocks, sacks of salt, heaps of dung or the bodies of the dead.

In a dark cove on the far, less-traveled side of the market was a flat-roofed, earthen enclosure with doors on four sides. Young girls with painted eyes leaned sensuously against its outer walls engaging momentarily with approaching men who came and went nervously from darkened doors.

In most open courts of the town, where broad roadways crossed, there were small, ornate wooden temples where worshippers of a local god could offer incense, say prayers or speak to a priest. By one such temple was a distinctive group of long-haired, half naked men of undeterminable age dressed only in orange skirts tied loosely at the waist. They were what townspeople called "holy men," religious ascetics, that kept strictly to themselves living on what they could garner from the passing crowd. They lingered at the side of the street engaging with the passing crowd. With a touch on the elbow they would humbly request to offer various magical services for a small fee. They were known as the Alya, named, it was said, after a star in the tail of the Scorpio star group. Their hair, of uncertain dark color, uncut and caked with animal dung, hung in tangled strands nearly to the back of their knees. Their feet were wrapped, not in leather sandals as most of that day, but in tattered woolen cloth. Their skin and waist cloth were soiled, intentionally it appeared, with ashes and dung, or something as putrid.

Townspeople avoided them, for obvious reasons, but the Alya were quick to spot travelers and the less street-wise from out of town over whom they could gain some advantage and offer their magic in whispered words of the spirit world and perform divinations. It was said they could, supernaturally, speak the names and birthplaces of ancestors and other things impossible to know.

The Alya had been driven, for reasons unknown, from a distant region beyond the western hills. They were looked upon locally with suspicion, because they belonged to no tribe or family. But they had acquired a place in this town and others by bribes and threats. There were other such mystery cults roaming the land.

Some claimed to have a connection to the otherworld, have the power to heal the sick, communicate with spirits, and escort souls of the dead to the afterlife. Virtually no one had no religious beliefs at all. Curses, demons, spirit visions and magic of all sorts seemed very real and the world of nature around them, itself, was just too full of mystery and wonder to be anything but the manifestation of deity of immense power and intelligent, living energy.

Noah's son Shem was once tempted by his own curiosity. Could these men really speak hidden things? Was this magic real? When he was a younger man on an errand in town, an Alya approached him. Fortunately, before he could bring a coin up out of his pocket to satisfy the itch in his spirit, brother Japheth saw him, and with a sharp word, took hold of Shem's tunic and pulled him away.

"Yes," Japheth said soberly, "he will tell you a hidden thing. Don't let him speak from the spirit world. It is playing with the serpent and with fire." Since then, as Shem learned more of the spirit world, he became aware that these things were dangerously real and to be shunned. He was indebted to Japheth, the older, more practical-minded brother who teased Shem often about being impressionable and naïve.

Altars of various sorts, some of stone, some of wood, some of gold, could be found here and there, sometimes in unexpected places. Places of worship in the city could be seen where empty sandals were lined up at some well-worn threshold, where aromatic smoke drifted from a doorway, where, on certain days there was unceasing chanting and charred remains of birds and animals lay smoldering in the ditch. It was a time of many beliefs and gods. At times a group would come to power who did not always allow certain other groups to exist freely. Noah had seen many strong men of valor rise to power, rule for a season, then be displaced by another. Usually, the powerful were of a certain cult, or were self-declared gods themselves, forbidding the alien beliefs, destroying sacred things and banishing the uncooperative.

36

The City Across the River

This sectarian, tribal exercise of power was the way of the land. People of the earth were led from peace to instability, either through outright force or through cleaver manipulation of information. Then, as the people became desperate for some form of order and they were left with no good choices, they submitted to a form of slavery in exchange for order.

In the decades before Noah's call from God to build the ark, conflicts between opposing groups had intensified. Violence against "undesirables" was encouraged. Certain stories and traditions were squashed by the ruling elite. What had been true was now declared false. A new ideal, touted as just and right was twisted into justification for inhuman, brutal treatment of others. One member of the community was encouraged to spy on another. It was not uncommon for a family member to disappear in the night.

Noah's ideals, his traditions and story handed down to him from the righteous forefathers, had been declared irrelevant, even offensive to the religious rulers of the city. The Creator God worshipped by Noah was considered distant, intransigent and unworthy of respect.

Noah's lands were part of the world divided along edges of streams, forests and ridges into tribal sectors, each with its own ruler and each having to defend its own interests. Though the descendants of Seth dreamed of a time of peaceful coexistence, it never came. Rulers combined forces for the purpose of mutual cooperation, but yet stronger forces combined and appeared on the horizon with spears in hand. Men were slain, strongmen thrown down and new boundaries drawn. It was a reality Noah had suffered all his life and each man on the street had his own solution, but no solution was found that prevailed.

Only a few years had passed since the last war. There had been decades of ambushes, sieges, peace deals and treachery. Keeping the peace was a long hard slog. The local ruler, at the time of this story, was hard as stone and more fearful than a lion. Neighbors from the east, miscalculated that they could storm the city walls, control the river and steal the local resources. They were destroyed as were many other unwelcome visitors. Repelling outsiders was a frequent task, often with much loss of life. There were always men of power looking for fresh lands to plunder. The only advantage to the town, a rather ironic one, was the many slaves acquired from captured enemies. They had become a very valuable source of labor to rebuild walls and prepare for the next siege.

They worked hard and were cooperative having no family, and little freedom to make choices.

Survival by spear and sword was not without great cost. Many of the local young men and women had been carted off and never again found, storehouses raided, the most elite force of mounted warriors utterly lost and the city's east wall left in ruins. But the town leader, nevertheless, managed to raise a force of a thousand men, many of them merchants and rivermen. Recently, they drove invaders back and pursued them all the way to their distant camp, burned it and left not a man, woman, child or beast alive.

This is how life was in those days. Peace came at a very high price. Violence, perversion and chaos reigned. The idea that, deep down, there was a heart of goodness in Man had long been abandoned. That fact had become frightfully obvious. It was strength against strength. Goodness was the soft, vulnerable underside of human nature.

9

The Call

On one particularly memorable day, Noah, as he often did, rose just before dawn, picked up his woven mat, passed through the gate at the rear of the compound and went to his private place of prayer.

There was a group of tall pines under which he had constructed a simple bench made of a wooden beam laid across two flat rocks. It faced west away from the outer wall of the compound. The first rays of the sun began to show in the dark sky. A breeze came in off the river and there was a soft sighing in the tops of the pines, Noah's favorite sound in the world. The daily mist that watered the land would soon be lifting. He rested there on the bench for a few moments.

He rolled out his mat on the carpet of needles and went down on his knees on the mat, his back to the compound. Looking up at the few bright stars that remained, he began to pray and to worship.

What made this day memorable, was that this particular prayer time became more of a listening time than his usual prayers, his usual practice of repeating words passed down to him from creation. What Noah heard that morning changed everything. The future of Noah's family and the fate of all the earth was decided right there on that woven mat. It had been decided in the heart of the Lord God, and was revealed to Noah in clear and surprisingly concise language.

God had become grieved that he had made Man on the earth. Every intention, every thought of every man's heart was toward evil. God's heart was filled with pain for he loved those whom he had created. In his sovereign will, he had decided to destroy everything and start again. And he would begin again with this humble old man on his knees before him. A flood would come upon the whole earth, all living creatures with breath would perish.

Then, he charged Noah with the specifics for a grand and incomprehensible project, an ark to save them all.

That evening, Noah and his wife, Nayiri, gathered their sons and the wives to meet around the evening fire. Everyone in the group could sense that there was going to be some sort of special announcement. Dispensing with the usual evening chatter, they all gave Noah their full attention.

"The Creator God has spoken to me," Noah began slowly. "He has told me things that he is going to do and things he wants us to do." Then before giving the details, he added, "This is going to test all of us. I need you to gather up all the faith and maturity you can muster. I want you to put your trust, not so much in me, but in God."

Everyone became a little uneasy looking around at the others.

"Father, when you say he spoke to you, what do you mean?" asked Ham. "Did you hear his voice? I mean did you. . . ."

"Ham!" Shem interrupted, "Please. Give father a chance to explain!"

Noah, stared into the fire, picked up a stick and began poking around in the red coals. "When I speak to you," he said, "you hear my voice, don't you? As when I am speaking to you now."

He looked at Ham. "Then, a moment later, you have my words in you, in your mind, but not my voice. It is like that with God, who is spirit. He speaks in a way I cannot explain, but his words remain in me. And I know it is him, because I have come to know him, which is to know his heart. I believe we are all created for the purpose of knowing him. And when we know him we know his voice. And when we do this often, faith and trust build up between the two of us and it becomes like walking. . .walking through life together."

"How do you know it is not your imagination?" Japheth asked in as non-confrontational voice as he could.

"When we dream, our minds can create many odd things, that is true. But when God speaks to me, it is not of my own will, but of his. What he has told me is very troubling and difficult to understand, but it is what he has said. I can only tell you that I know his voice and I know what he said."

"And let me tell you this," he went on, "you will never be content and live out your true purpose in this life, until you learn to hear what the Lord is telling you and believe in your heart that he will accomplish his word spoken to us and to our fathers."

Nayiri looked around quickly at the group and then fixed her eyes on her husband as though she was speaking for all of them. She was obviously very concerned.

"Noah, tell us exactly what God said and maybe we can sort out what this means. Please!"

"Yes my dear. I love you all and respect your opinions, but what he has said is not negotiable. We cannot presume to instruct the Creator. God has spoken and we will obey. Keep in mind what has been revealed to us from the beginning, that he is *good*. He looked at what he created and saw that it was very good, therefore his will and his ways are good and just, for there can be no justice without goodness and no goodness without justice. God does not change. So, his will and intentions toward us are without even a trace of ill will. There is no cruelty in him. Most importantly, and we stake everything on this, his words are true. All men may be liars. But God is truth itself. Don't forget that."

"I am convinced," Noah went on in a quieter voice, "he has a plan to save humanity, to redeem the corrupt world through what he is about to do, even though it may appear his power is used against us. Remember what he spoke to the serpent? 'The offspring of the woman will crush your head!' Whose head? The deceiver's head. Sin's head. Death's head. That is a most precious promise of hope given to all humanity. This 'offspring of the woman' is our future hope, our only hope. And, the project I am going to tell you about, is part of that plan."

"Ok," his wife said, "Tell us what he said to you."

And he went on to repeat, word for word what God had told him.

God told Noah he was going to put an end to the people he had created and destroy the earth itself, because all was corrupt and filled with violence. He said it was not just some corruption, but all, every being, was corrupt in all their ways. Noah was to build a wooden ark, a kind of vessel which would hold his family, male and female members of every animal family and enough food to sustain them. He dictated the exact measurements and specified the basic design of the vessel. It was to be of a certain wood, have a door, a roof, three decks and be coated inside and out with pitch.

He promised to establish a covenant with Noah before they entered the completed ark. He would then send a flood to cover every part of the earth under heaven. All life, everything with breath, every creature that moves upon the ground, the Creator said, will be destroyed.

There was a long pause. Shem and Japheth stared at their father. Ham sat looking into the fire. Some of the wives covered their faces with their hands and quietly cried.

"My dear ones," Noah said softly, "I say it again, our Lord God is good. It is he who made the heavens and the earth and everything in them. And it is he who has authority over all. We all know the darkness of this world, the terror that threatens us every night, each time we move outside these walls. We know the beasts that prey on us and on each other, the endless war among men, the hatred all have toward the ways of God. Can we accuse God of having wrong motives? No. He did not tempt Eve to sin. He is not the author of lawlessness. He is the *giver* of life! He breathed into Man the breath of life so that we may walk in relationship to him. He made us to be like him, not like arrogant beasts!"

Noah leaned forward and looked around at their faces. "Can we trust him?"

Starting with Shem, they slowly, one by one, began to nod in the affirmative.

"*Will* we obey him? Or will we turn to our own ways, as Eve and all mankind has so wickedly done?"

Again, there was a pause. They all knew that Noah, now nearly five-hundred years old, had a long and special relationship with the Creator God and no one there in the circle doubted his sincerity. There was an unmistakable power, a kind of living force in his words. He had increasingly demonstrated a humility that engendered trust. His force of character was recognized, even by his many enemies. Unlike the officials of the city and the warlords that ruled the land, he did not command others through threats and intimidation. And, in those days of constant danger, his defense was not the strength of arms, high stone walls or a troop of brutish body guards, but strength of spirit. Many times over his long life he had overcome man and beast by inner strength, an unseen force. He had often repeated the phrase, "The Lord is my keeper in the time of trouble."

Each member of the family received the challenge of this shocking revelation in his or her own way, some with a rising sense of excitement for being singled out by the Creator to take on a great mission and some with a choking sense of fear.

Ham was the first to speak.

"What is a flood?"

They all laughed, but Ham was serious.

"Yeah, and what is an ark?" Japheth added.

None of them, except Noah, had seen the ocean or witnessed a flood. They knew only the waters of rivers, lakes

and ponds, flat-bottomed river barges and boats used in shallow waters.

Rivers, at that time, followed the gentle contour of the land and were fed from springs welling up from the deep far beyond the hills. Each morning a mist descended on most areas, especially the lower, cooler elevations, bringing moisture to all living things. Never, since creation, had enough water fallen from the heavens or risen from the deep to cause waters to overflow more than enough to form seasonal pools.

There was no word in their language for the deluge Noah was talking about. A flood, to them, was the filling of a cattle feed trough, a wife throwing out the waste water, the opening of an irrigation ditch. Those were floods. This flood of judgement was something else, something new and unfathomable.

"How did this vision come to you, father?" asked Shem.

Noah explained how he had been at his place on the pathway, early in the morning. He felt the special presence of God and couldn't help but kneel and bow low onto his woven mat.

"When God said, 'I am going to put an end to all people,'" Noah said, "I wondered if I heard correctly. It didn't make sense. He was the Lord of Creation and had the sovereign power and the right to do as he wished. But it is he who had breathed into Man the breath of life and had created the world we live in and it seemed contrary to his will that it be destroyed. Yet, he was speaking and I listened."

"Then God described the ark, the dimensions, the details. It didn't make sense. At first, I saw a small barge in my limited imagination, but when God told me the dimensions, I began to realize the tremendous size. Over one hundred and fifty paces long and twenty-five paces wide! And as high as a tall pine! Fear came over me. Then, I had a kind of conversation with God and received assurance that he would supply our needs and give direction. I called out to him, asked questions and prayed for understanding. I could see the vessel in my mind's eye, couldn't understand it, but I could see it. There has never been such a thing.

"We can be sure that the Lord God will provide a way of escape for us. This ark is a way of salvation. We may fear. We may not understand, but we can be sure of his word. He is not so weak or distant that he cannot save us."

"That is going to have to be very true," Japheth said. "We are going to need a strong and very present helper if we are to build this. . .this monstrosity!"

On that note of agreement, the group rose and went, each to their own dwelling. Before Shem could take more than a few steps Noah approached him and brought him to the side.

With a rather sheepish, apologetic look on his face, Noah said, "Shem, actually, what worried me the most is how you would react to all this. Because, I need you, especially you, if we are to obey and carry out the Creator's demands. I cannot do this myself. Shem, I am going to have to lean heavily upon your willingness to grow in knowledge of God. I see something special in you. I need you to cast this vision to the others and to help them to not lose heart."

Of course, when word got out, there was a temporary panic. Rumors spread among servants that Noah had had some sort of mental breakdown. He was an eccentric character and often spoke of things difficult to comprehend. But now, he was talking nonsense about destruction of the earth, the end of all people and the construction of a gigantic, floating object called an "ark." There was deep respect for Noah, but this was incomprehensible.

When rumors drifted across the river into town, officials at the highest level began to speak again of eliminating this troublesome Noah and gaining control of his lands and his wealth.

10

The Preparations

In the far-distant future skeptics may smile and wonder about this story, about this Noah. How could it be true that this primitive, five-hundred-year-old man, who lacked the sophisticated tools and know-how of a more technologically advanced age, could accomplish the impossible task he had been called to do. There were just so many things he didn't have compared to builders of the future. But skeptics are seldom persons of great vision and have difficulty understanding how inspiration overcomes the impossible. A person with great vision doesn't fret about what he *doesn't* have. He gets on with the task at hand using what he *does have*.

Noah may have been old and may have had comparatively simple tools, but the truth is, he had intellectual capacity and agility of mind that would stun and confound a man of a more modern age. Having been born relatively soon after Adam, he had the advantage of living during the very early stages of life on Earth before sin's corrosive impact had degraded the environment. Genetically, he was relatively undamaged. He, as others of his time, had a clear mind and possessed immense mental capacity, problem solving ability and memory. He was intimately familiar with his environment and knew how to use it. And, his longevity was not a detriment. Rather, Noah had accumulated a vast store of knowledge over centuries of experience. It was common during his time to live several hundred years before the aging effect of cosmic rays and pollution on human cells finally brought death. Before the flood, a layer of water vapor in the upper atmosphere may have shielded him and all other living creatures from cell-damaging rays. The soil was cleaner and the air was nearly pristine. A more modern person can only dream of having the clarity and brilliance of Noah.

As he famously once said to a young, cocky wood-fitter, "Young man, I've *forgotten* more about wood-fitting than you *know*!"

Even among the great men of his day, Noah was well known for his sharp mind and well-honed skills. Known in ages to come as builder of the ark, he was, actually, and by nature, a man of the soil, a planter. He knew more than any in the region about seeds, planting, grafting, pruning, harvesting and which crops were best for health and profit. In addition, he could call upon his skills to build and design using wood, stone, bronze and iron. He had not been idle during the previous five-hundred years. He taught himself intricate wood joining techniques and methods of handling heavy materials. He was inquisitive and inventive becoming familiar with spinning hemp fiber into rope, forging metals, using hoists, drying timber, selecting quality trees and knowing how to dry and season wood. He had learned from the master of a quarry in the distant north how to use gravity to lift stones of many tons into place, sometimes positioning them on pillars three times the height of a man. He knew things that have mystified more modern men. He had built the market place in the town center. He was a successful builder before the call of God to build the ark. He built the largest local meeting hall in the city with raised stone platforms for entertainers, dancers, athletes and spectators. And, of course, he oversaw the development of his compound with all its various buildings and functions.

It was not possible to thrive in the days of Noah, in a violent, chaotic culture without an insightful, gifted mind. Wealth usually follows power, but in Noah's case, it followed brilliance, ingenuity and tenacity. Noah would deny it was because of his own cleverness. He believed the hand of a merciful Creator God was on his life from his early days granting him direction and favor.

The time finally came for work on the ark to begin. The vision had been communicated and, as much as possible, the initial questions had been answered. Fears and doubts remained, especially among the servants. And there was a nearly infinite list of unknowns. But Noah had made it clear that disobeying the Creator's command, and therefore his own commands, was not an option. Once they had looked each other in the face, done the customary ritual of establishing a covenant, they were agreed to move forward. They were bound to one another in a common venture. There was to be no murmuring or second guessing. Too much was at stake.

The back, western wall of the compound was extended outward to include a flat, stony field large enough to easily place the ark and all the stockpiles of materials needed. The field was adjacent to a bend in the river where the water was deep enough and the bank shaped in such a way as to provide a good landing place for materials coming by barge. Preparing the field, upgrading the landing and making ready took the better part of the first year.

Shem and Japheth spent many days with their father going over the precise instructions given to Noah. They had the raw dimensions, but since this would be a floating vessel of enormous size, they had to admit their knowledge of barges and river fishing craft was insufficient.

So, while Japheth and Ham were preparing the field and landing, Noah took Shem on an extended trip to the coastal lands where they spent many days observing the shape and form of many different kinds of vessels meant to operate in the wild waters of the ocean. The sea-going vessels of the day did not roam far from shore, but they had been experimenting for centuries with the design, materials and building techniques.

Shem was especially fascinated with the subtle design differences between various vessels used for heavy hauling. He asked each sea captain many questions about what specific features had been developed which kept the vessel upright and stable in rough water. He took careful note also of the inner structure, deck supports and methods used to seal the craft. He was able to judge the current state of the art of watercraft of his time. Having studied vessels up and down the coast, Noah and Shem were anxious to pass on this knowledge to Japheth and Ham.

Shem and Noah were impressed with a particularly large vessel which had survived heavy seas without any of the serious problems encountered by others. But the captain, a sun-burned brute of a man, was slow to volunteer information. When he was convinced that these two visitors were from far away, he reluctantly shared details, but asked them not to tell others. He had devised a way to perfect a sea-going hull, made of overlapping, bowed planks, joined with iron spikes and caulked in such a way to increase safety as well as to give the craft added buoyancy. He explained how to bend specially hewn planks over hot coals and how to build forms to shape the hot planks to precise and repeatable dimensions. The captain knew exactly what weight of cargo he could safely take onboard, where to position heavy loads and he knew the angle to which the craft would tip before she would right herself. The old captain gave Noah a toothless grin and said proudly, "She'll take me safely through the most wicked waters, she will!"

Then he added, "Sounds like you're building something pretty big. That'll take some doing. What kind of cargo exactly do you plan to carry?"

Shem shrugged and Noah answered, "A good number of livestock and such." And they left it at that. As they walked away, Noah put his arm around Shem's shoulders, pulled him close and whispered, "God sent that man to us!"

They knew they had the best sea-going vessel technology of their day and began their journey home with an increased sense of confidence in the ark design that was forming in their heads. This was an exciting point in the whole process of building an ark for these two visionaries. In a very real sense, as they traveled along together, they were building the ark bit by bit in the eyes of their minds, sharing with each other their ideas and adding to the design as various aspects were accepted or rejected. But, they were not so naïve to think there would be no problems. There was still much to be worked out.

For the rest of their lives, Noah and Shem would remember those days, riding along together on the backs of donkeys, as the gloriously creative time when God inspired them with the special knowledge needed to build an object so extraordinary that it would mystify all peoples for ages to come.

The day after arriving back at the compound Noah called for what he called, "a pause to worship." In their language it meant literally "to go up" as in smoke. An earthen altar was built and a young calf was offered as a whole burnt offering to provide what Noah called, "a sweet aroma to the Lord." As the family and servants gathered around Noah he explained that the entire offering would be consumed with nothing left for anyone to eat as in other offerings. This, he said, was to signify their total commitment to the Lord God and to the work to which they had been called. This was the first step on a long journey which would consume their energies for a century.

That evening there was a friendly gathering of the entire community around tables of food and the very best wines.

"We are going to do the impossible," Noah told them raising a cup. "There will be opposition and we will face challenges beyond our ability to solve. But the Lord God has called us and he will show us the way! Already he has shown us how to begin. We must only be willing to follow. We will not rely on our own understanding, but on his power to accomplish the impossible!"

With that, the entire gathering of over a hundred souls, let out a tremendous cheer that carried in the evening air over the river and was heard in the city market place and beyond alerting the officials that something was stirring in Noah's camp.

The worship time and the celebration took the entire day from morning to long after sundown. Everyone was tired, especially Noah and Shem, still recovering from their long journey. But the burnt offering to the Lord and Noah's priestly words had a mysteriously encouraging effect and a very peaceful spirit filled the camp. The day of worship helped dispel the tension that had been mounting while Noah and Shem had been away. Some of the sense of dread had lifted as they were reminded of the Creator's presence and power to save.

Now, it was time to go to work.

Did you know? – *Fine woodworking and craftsmanship are found in some of the most ancient tombs of Egypt. Mortise and tenon joints, delicate inlays and design and a very high level of knowledge about drying and curing woods was prevalent in the far distant past. The ancients have demonstrated the capacity to handle extremely massive and complex projects through sheer brilliance and marvelous ingenuity.*

11

The Plan

Noah and Shem sat down with Japheth to describe to him the plan. Japheth would be called on to begin construction. He was a natural fit to oversee the crews that would do the work. Shem, with his intuitive sense of design and his ability to visualize the end product, would be asked to convey plans to the others as needed and work with Japheth to manage the project. Ham, had already made it clear he was happy to leave the details to the older brothers and was more than ready to pick up an axe and go to work when the time came.

He was also prepared to contact his network of skilled laborers in the city.

Japheth was still having a very hard time getting his mind around the whole concept.

And, Japheth was having doubts.

"Listen Japheth," Noah told him before going over the plans, a bit irritated, "the Creator was very specific in laying out the dimensions of this thing. So, I'm going to depend on you to work with Shem and to sort out the details and to begin figuring out how it is going to be done. You are the practical one. I need you!"

"Yes." Japheth answered. "And that is what I am trying to be. Practical! Father, this *thing*, as you call it, has never before existed! There is no use for such a thing. We can build it. Yes. But to float such a vessel of that size would take more water than. . .well, than anyone has seen in the history of this world!"

Noah nodded and smiled. "Yes, but this is a *God thing*. And it will float in water God will send. Impractical to us, yes, but sensible to him, therefore sensible to me. Our task is to use our minds and hands to build what we have been told to build. The mystery part will unveil itself in due time."

Then, in a softer voice, Noah added, "I know. It doesn't make sense. But, I know it was God's word to me. Already he has shown us how to begin. Here, let us show you."

The three squatted down and Noah smoothed out a spot of dry dirt with the palm of his hand. He took a small stick and drew a box-shaped object and then, pointing to each line, spoke the dimensions, 510 feet long, 85 feet wide and 51 feet high. Three decks. The roof was to be about a foot and a half above the upper deck. All would be sealed with pitch, inside and out. They needed room to take onboard a pair of every kind of animal and enough provisions for them all. And there would have to be a place for the family.

"These are the basic instructions," he said.

Japheth scratched his bearded chin for a long moment, took the stick and rounded the bottom corners of the box.

"Father, if this is going to go in large waters, larger even than you have seen in the great sea, I don't think it should be flat bottomed as our river barges. A rounded bottom would roll better in deep water. This ark is high, as well as wide, so

57

weight must rest in the bottom, then, when it tips to the side, the wider top edge will cause it to right itself. I have seen this principle in small boats used by fishermen.".

Noah and Shem both burst out laughing, startling Japheth. Shem pushed Japheth back on his hands in the dirt.

"You!" Shem yelled at him laughing. "The one who doubts but has already grasped and understood so much! You understand what father and I traveled far and worked so hard to understand!"

Noah reached out a hand and helped Japheth to his feet, then grabbed him around the neck with one arm, raised his other arm and said with great emotion, "Thank you! Thank you for Japheth. Thank you for providing all we need to do what you have asked us to do!"

They continued working out problems, keeping to the prescribed dimensions. They talked about how they could construct a door on the side, how pitch would be applied inside and out and other details.

"Why is the roof to be a foot and a half above the sides, father?"

Noah smiled, "I think you will know the answer to that question after a few days living with a thousand critters!"

They could only guess at how long this project would take. It would take many years. And they were not at all sure how they were going to perform the thousand tasks needed to even begin to complete a vision never before conceived. But there was, at this first planning session, a sense of excitement as Japheth began to see the project take shape in his mind. He was, at this early stage, content to have his rather predictable life shaken up. And Ham was anxious to impress, as youngest, to show his family what he could do.

When Noah returned to Nayiri that evening, the two of them didn't sleep so well. There was just so much to lay there and think about. Secretly, they were fighting fears and insecurities that older people sometimes have and were feeling overwhelmed.

Did you know? – *The proportions of Noah's ark, given in the Bible in the Book of Genesis, are still the basic proportions used by ship builders today. The length-to-width ratio is approximately the perfect ratio for transporting loaded vessels in heavy seas.*

12

Laying Out the Ark

It took months for Noah and the three brothers to come to full agreement on the plans. Anxious to begin, Noah sometimes pushed the planning harder than he should and there were tense moments when conversations came to an abrupt end, tempers flared, apologies given and the work begun again. In addition, there were field crops, orchards and vineyards to tend to, venders to pay and the daily duties of running a compound. So, like any project, especially a large complicated one, it was hard to draw a final line on the plan and to commence the actual work. The brothers were still trying to grasp the responsibilities assigned to them. While Shem and Japheth were planning the ark, Ham was planning to make contacts in the city and meet with river barge captains.

Finally, the day came when Noah said, "Ok. Enough thinking and preparing. I want to begin laying it out."

The very next day, Japheth and Noah went out to the building field with an armload of wooden stakes and a large bundle of hemp cord. They paced off exactly 510 feet down the center of the field starting as close to the river landing as possible. They drove a stout stake at each end and connected them with a tightly stretched cord. This would be the most fundamental central line of the ark from which all other lines would be measured. It would determine the length and true straightness of the vessel, something the old sea captain had called "tracking."

They expected that, at some point, they might need to employ some means of navigation, maybe some form of rudder. If this line was not carefully used as a true guide, the vessel would veer annoyingly one way or the other. They laid out a dozen or so stakes at right angles to this line defining the width and curved shape of the vessel front to back, the widest mid-point being exactly 85 feet wide. This was all done according to the Creator's instructions and the detailed plan they had agreed upon.

It was a small beginning, a mere two-dimensional hint of what was to rise from the ground, a faint image of that ethereal ark that existed vaguely in the minds of Noah and Shem. Putting the stakes in, stretching the cord and standing back to see the layout was an auspicious moment for Noah who could not stop going on and on about it to Nayiri, telling her multiple times every detail of what they had done. He chattered excitedly all through their evening meal and beyond, until she had to tell him to kindly be quiet or he would have to sleep on the porch.

Over the next few months materials were stockpiled near the building site and the tool house was busy forging cutting tools, spikes and rods of both iron and bronze. A building normally used for storing animal feed was repurposed as a wood working shop for the smaller components of the ark, such as spindles, crates, pegs, gates, troughs and stair treads. Workers began to construct several, large bow-turning lathes for producing the many pegs and spindles that would be needed. The massive frame beams, the heavy plank decking and the overlapping boards of the hull of the ark would be dried, split and hewn to shape in the field. Nearly every part of this massive craft was over-sized. The scale of it was larger than what any of these men had worked on or even seen before. When Noah and Shem designed it, they had tried to estimate the vast number of winged and furry passengers they were expecting, animals which would need cages, feeding, bedding, waste removal and watering systems. Most of these details were already in the plan but much would have to be worked out as they went. A lot of innovation and brainstorming was going to happen throughout the project, but everyone knew there would have to be very particular accommodations made for pairs of a broad variety of passengers of every kind, large, small, flying, creeping, crawling and human, if they were to survive what was coming.

13

The Wood

The wood used to build the ark was specified in Noah's instructions, but there's no sense in troubling the reader with the name of the tree, because it may not grow in his or her area, especially since the flood. The waters that came and the upheaval of the rocks changed the earth's surface. The change is more than can be imagined. Nothing is the same. The sun, moon and stars still shine. Otherwise, all has changed.

Where there were plains, there are now majestic edifices of rock that have pushed their way up from the deep to ascend into the clouds. These jagged, belching mountains are new. Where there was sea, now there is land. And the land is divided into many lands and many seas. Realms of the world that were once steamy and lush and inhabited by giant creatures are now gone, covered by miles of rock and mud heaved up and over all by the receding water of the flood. The hill country, the river, the northern fountains, the crystal lake that fed the rivers, the vast green plains that were Noah's lands, the cities and the delta, all are gone. No one can know today, many years later, even where any of these places were.

In their hearts flood survivors want to know where their home once was, or where Eden might have been, or the place where God walked with Adam and Eve, or where their sacred traditions began. But, they really cannot know for God has begun anew and so shall they. Even the daily dew that they so depended on, the moisture that never failed to water their lands, is no longer. The sky itself seems different, more blue, more clear. Now, after those years when smoke and darkness covered the earth after the flood, the sun seems brighter than ever before making what was cool, cold, and what was once warm, hot. Even shadows seem different.

But more about how that all happened later.

As for the type of wood, Noah's wife called it "the broom tree." She, and others of her time, bundled its wispy greenery at the ends of its branches to make brooms. Each day, a servant girl would use the brooms to sweep and smooth the dirt walking paths around the compound.

As one could assume, the wood prescribed by God turned out to be the perfect wood for the ark. It was medium hard wood of a tall, straight tree that grew in dense groves and had a rather streaky, light color. It grew in abundance down river in the marshy areas near the delta where the river flowed into the sea. Its most desirable quality was its ability to endure moisture, bugs and mold. The building location was rather dry, but the project took a long time and to everyone's relief, the wood withstood the test of time. It remained sound all through the long years of building. The question was, would it perform when it was given the ultimate test of tests?

Another feature of this wood was, it could be split or cut using the tools of the time. Ham, working with skilled laborers, using sharp stone, iron and bronze axes and wedges, could split great logs into flat planks. Dwellings and many structures in town were made using the same techniques. The art of making interlocking wooden joints, as mentioned earlier, had long been used to make fine chairs, boxes and all sorts of furnishings.

The main problem was getting the raw logs many miles up from the delta, against the river's current. It was the first major challenge. It would be expensive and could be done only during the harvest season when waters ran low and barges could move against lesser currents. The family had, for many years, employed rivermen and their teams of oxen to pull barges loaded with materials upstream from the delta. But when Ham told the river boss the size and quantity needed, the big man slapped his forehead and stared at him, cursed and spat. Then, after Ham revealed what Noah was willing to pay, he envisioned a pile of gold coins, and became, suddenly, very agreeable. Brother Japheth, being a woodsman and a tough negotiator, demanded that he travel to the logging site on the delta to personally select the logs.

In those times, no one could trust rivermen. They were notorious swindlers.

14

The Town Workers

The family was slow to engage in contracts with anyone in those days, especially rivermen, unless the need was urgent. Venders or tradesmen seldom kept their promises. This break-down in trust was evident everywhere. Everyone carried some form of defense, some tool of protection. From every person's belt hung a pouch for personal valuables, a smaller pouch with a fire tool and pitch, and a dagger. Some kind of sharp instrument, usually home-made, was tucked into the belt in plain sight across from the right hand where it could be quickly put to use, either to slice an apple or someone's face. Even women moving through the crowds in the market kept weapons ready beneath a fold of their garment. The days when a person felt safe enough to walk around indifferent to surroundings had passed. When a sharp verbal warning wasn't enough, a person had to have both the nerve to use physical force and the quickness to make it stick. The number of daily violent encounters had risen to the point where rules against such things were ignored and rarely enforced.

Judges and law enforcers had become so weary with the load of cases, most had quit. Only the wealthy could protect themselves because they had a troop of armed guards.

It wasn't exactly anarchy, where everyone was on guard against everyone else, because group membership offered some order and security. There were clans and religious sects, each with its own armed security force ready to exact swift revenge on anyone daring to harm one of its members. So, there was a kind of safety in numbers within these groups if you were a clearly recognized member. Distinctively colored tunics, sashes or turbans were worn for identification. It was important to remain in good standing with your group. To offend one's own group, to be kicked out or banished was a fearful thing.

Members of Noah's family, when in town, wore the distinctive pale red turban with a distinctive gold cord wound into it. Noah's ability to take care of his own was well known. It was not a pleasant thing to fall into his hands. The old man was pious and had old-fashioned ideas, but it was not a good idea to harm one of his own or betray his confidence. He may not stick you with a dagger, but ultimately he would cause you to bitterly regret your sin against him.

With the increasing chaos of those times, before the flood, men had become especially self-protective and cunning. When you combine that with physical bodies that were strong and agile, it made for a violent combination. Trained from childhood to defend themselves or their interests, they were light and quick, as a rule, rather than thick and strong. In mind and body they were prepared more for street fighting than for hard, demanding manual work that required thought and patience.

Nevertheless, Noah needed laborers, cynical and brutish or not. He sent Ham into the city to find them.

The first task was to dig out a rounded pit under the central line, which was of roughly the shape and form of the hull. This was Ham's idea. The pit would minimize the height of the project and help give support to massive ribs of the vessel as they were laid into place. Ham put a crew of common laborers to work with picks and shovels. Shem checked on the progress daily to see that they were shaping the pit properly.

After some weeks, Noah was encouraged to see the shape of the vessel appearing in the ground.

During that time Japheth traveled downstream to the delta to select and oversee the loading of the first batch of broom tree logs. Several barges were loaded. Oxen, driven along by barking rivermen, began their tedious upstream journey along the river bank pulling on heavy lines attached to the barges.

After days of travel upstream, as the barges passed under the bridge between the city and the compound, Japheth turned over the docking and unloading to Ham's city crew. There was a scuffle at the landing as the rivermen, exhausted and irritable from a long haul, argued over money being exchanged. Barges were tied up at the building field landing and an armed guard was posted over the site as Ham instructed his team of workers where and how to stack the timbers, beams and planks on land.

15

The Stress

Upon returning home with the logs, Japheth sat at his mother's table and looked at his two brothers. His mother had just placed before them three earthenware cups of the fermented juice of apples and a still-warm-from-the-oven, hard-crusted loaf of bread. Japheth took a cup in a bandaged hand, drank from it, then unfolded the bandage for his brothers to see the wound.

"It's not getting any easier out there to work with them." he said. "This is how I am repaid for giving them our business." The brothers leaned forward over the rough-hewn table looking at the dark, crusted gash in Japheth's palm.

"It could have been worse," Ham said, taking just a quick glance, having plenty of scars of his own.

That morning, rivermen had refused to onload the barges until they were paid and Japheth had given half-payment and agreed to pay the other half when logs were stacked on shore. There was an outburst of profanity and a spear was thrust forward from the group of men catching Japheth in the hand.

Shem watched as Japheth wrapped the cloth back around his hand and said, "This is a problem we are going to have to solve either by force or diplomacy. And, obviously, force isn't going to work. We are going to need those rivermen, all of them, clear down to the delta and upstream to the timberland. I told them specifically that payment would be made when logs were delivered and stacked on dry land at our landing. That was clear."

"Once we get the wood to the landing, our oxen teams can get it to the clearing." Ham added. They discussed further ways to obtain cooperation from river workers and the possibility of having to call in some favors from city officials to put some political pressure on the river bosses.

They decided to take the matter to their father, Noah, who could deal with Narek, the one man who had gained authority over use of the river, not only along the stretch near their city, but all of the river south of the city. Narek was on the ruling council of the city and had gained much wealth and power by slowly, over many years, capturing control of the commerce that came by barge. As the city grew, his influence had grown and there were very few who dared to defy him. Most of the city's goods came by caravan, but salt, raw minerals, stone and timber came by barge.

The three brothers were still trying to adjust to the increased demands and scope of the project their father, Noah, had revealed to them. They were grown men with wives and knew how to work. But this project, this daunting vision had stirred up in them emotions of anxiety as well as adventure, as the shear immensity of it weighed on them. They could only imagine the burden of their father. He was holding up well, but they could see the stress had taken its toll.

Along with the planning, designing and preparing came the awkward, even dangerous, task of explaining to people what they were building and why they were building it. No one, outside their family truly understood and cooperated unless there was profit in it. In fact, the three had given up explaining to people why they needed this beam or that forged iron spike. They volunteered information on a need-to-know basis. They often played on the expedience of human greed. By whatever means necessary, they kept the work going.

16

The Inner Struggle

From the beginning of the project, when Noah came to a major problem, he took it to his bench, his special place under the pines. He put it before God, then, when he felt he had God's mind on the matter, wouldn't be easily dissuaded. For the others, Noah's firm resolve was, at times, frustrating. But over time, they saw a definitely divine kind of power working through Noah's faith. He had his rough side, and he could get abrasive, but he truly was a unique character. When others saw the impossible, Noah tended to see an opportunity. He seemed always ready to see God do something impossible. But even in this staunch resolve, there was a brokenness, a readiness to acknowledge his own weakness.

Shem used the word "fearful," because being on that sharp edge between victory and disaster, which was quite often, he experienced both fear and joy. He had to admit, mostly fear. When afraid he'd think of how Noah would often hold up his hand, spread his five fingers and point to them. "Shem, if God can make *this*," he'd say wiggling his hand, "he can do *this*," and he'd point to the impossible task they were dealing with. If God can create a hand, he can surely show them how to fix the problem, whether it be joining massive wooden beams, or overcoming a dangerously corrupt official. He just never backed down.

Early on, Noah met with the city officials, explained what the ark was for and told them about God's judgement that was going to come. They did not receive the news well. One of the chief rulers told Noah, "You are mad! This is utter foolishness."

It is said that Noah responded, "The foolishness of God is wiser than the wisdom of man."

Word got around that Noah had lost touch with reality and people were advised not to support the project in any way. At some point, Shem asked him, "Our neighbors in town are squawking about our ark project and seriously offended by what you've said, that the judgement of God is coming. How can we deal with them without offending them?"

"When we offend someone by doing something wrong," Noah said, "then we should apologize and make things right. But if we offend someone because we are doing right, what is the will of God, and our conscience is clean, then we have no responsibility to satisfy them. Even if they think we're crazy! If we spend our days thinking how we shall satisfy and not offend, especially in this evil day, then we must wonder if we are offending the Lord God."

Noah went on, "Shem, we are going to be competing for resources of labor and materials. We are going to be dominating use of river barges and maybe we will be driving up prices of a lot of materials. People will find offense in everything we do and say. But, we are only doing what God told us to do and delivering the message given to us by God. They need to make a choice. Will they submit to him, join us in the ark and be saved? Or, will they not? We will move forward with what we know we must do, regardless of the resistance. Remember what God told Cain? He said, 'If you do not do what is right, sin is crouching at the door.' Shem, sin is very real and it desires to have us and wants to rule over us to keep us from doing what is right. No. We shouldn't waste time trying to appease this sinful generation. We will press on with what God has given us to do."

17

Beginning to Build

It was an exciting day when actual, physical construction began. The thinking and planning would continue, but the rough-cut broom wood beams were finally being pulled by ox teams to the building field.

Weeks before wood arrived at the compound, trees had been felled near the delta and made into rough-cut beams making transporting and handling much simpler. This was a skill of which there were few masters, even in that day when manual skills were exceedingly perfected.

The tallest, straightest broom trees had been selected by Japheth, felled with an iron axe and cut into twelve-foot sections. The ends were squared off and the logs were "cribbed" by lifting them unto a low flat work platform and fastened by iron spikes called "dogs" to keep them secure. While the tree was still green and easiest to work with, workmen stripped off the bark, measured each log determining the maximum size and number of beams it would yield, and drew chalk lines on the log to guide the axe-men who would hew it into beams and planks. These muscular "hewers" were respected men of great skill, strength and tenacity. It was rough and dangerous work swinging sharp, broad bladed hewing axes to carve out from the raw log smooth, straight beams Japheth had ordered.

This was done by cutting notches along the side of the log perpendicular to the ground every two feet. The material between the notches was then removed two feet at a time by laying the flat edge of the hewing axe against the wood and shaving out the waste wood until what remained was a flat, smooth and plumb surface. The dogs which held the log were removed, the log turned and the process repeated until a four-sided beam of desired size was finished.

These raw beams were transferred to rivermen and loaded onto barges, secured and pulled upstream.

The wood then became the responsibility of Japheth who was careful to keep inventory of what was needed and what was arriving. Ham's crew drew from these stockpiles of raw lumber to produce the parts that Shem asked for as he roamed the pit overseeing the actual construction. Noah presided over it all roaming from pit, to forge, to labor house, to landing with encouragement or advice. He could also be found at home each afternoon with his feet up, resting.

The first, very major challenge was laying the long sequence of connected beams that would be the central keel at the bottom of the ark to which the curving ribs would be attached. Even the largest broom trees could not produce a beam large enough for this keel, so multiple, heavy beams were bound together with massive iron straps, each one interlocking with others in a rigid unit which itself had to conform to the curved profile of the pit. This single unit, more than a hundred and fifty paces long, took a full year to construct. It tested the family's management skills. It tested

Ham's ability to keep laborers at the task. It tested Noah's patience. The entire keel project had multiple problems, mistakes, start-overs and moments when the brothers thought that even the All-Wise God had asked them to do the undoable.

But, having begun in the middle, they finally connected the last beams at the bow and the stern. And, they had laid in the connecting pieces, notched into the keel in sixty places, where the upward curving ribs would be attached. What they had at this point looked, from the edge of the pit, like a giant backbone pulled from a giant fish. Looking down the length of it, Shem and Japheth could see it was straight and true, properly curved and of right proportion. The vision of Noah and Shem was slowly, painstakingly taking shape.

Next came the ribs that would arch upward on each side of the ark to the height more than twenty times the height of a man. These were necessarily very thick and stout at the bottom where they connected to the keel, tapering to the top. Near the keel they were cut to shape, then fastened using the mortise and tendon technique that had been used for centuries to build their furniture and living structures. The legs on their four-legged woven beds were fastened this way. Their word *mortise* meant "to fasten," and their word *tenon* meant "to hold." The end of a beam was cut to form a tenon which fit snuggly into a pocket, then a peg or wedge was driven in to tighten the very solid joint. This was the primary system which held together all of the many parts of the ark. The large joints on large, structural beams were performed in the field near the site. The smaller fittings, such as for decking, partitions, railings or shelving were done in the work house wood-fitting shop where workers had benches, vises and special tools for precise work.

Smoke drifted over the compound on most days from the charcoal fires of Noah's forge. Several men and boys worked in the hot and noisy metal shop shaping red hot iron into spikes, straps, bars and tools needed for the ark. Ham, himself, could be found often at the forge. It was Ham who had the connections with vendors who dealt in minerals coming by caravan or barge from the mines of the northern hills. He hired metal specialists from the city to provide the know-how to produce the things needed. Nuggets of tin and copper were piled in heaps on the floor next to piles of raw iron ore, sand for molds and other minerals waiting to be dumped into the blazing hot cauldrons and melted and mixed according to knowledge of the day.

One sweaty worker coated in coal dust could be seen cutting iron rods and shaping the pieces into spikes. Another could be seen pounding red hot iron into an axe head, then squelching the hissing head into a wooden water barrel. Steam rose in a cloud cut by shafts of sunlight from the window. Another was working at a sharpening stone putting fine edges on the broad axes used to shape and trim wooden beams. Young boys, probably bond servants of one of the foundrymen, walked all day in a circle pulling against the spokes of a turnstile which drove wooden gears attached to levers which worked the billows which blew air into the hot coals under the brick oven and forge. Most of the inhabitants of the city grew up as these boys did, as either bond servants, slaves or children of slaves. Many of Ham's workers were not free citizens. That was the way it was then and had been for as long as anyone could remember.

Over a period of years, the ribs, supported by scaffolding, rose from the keel at the center of the pit, up the sides and into the air from head to tail end. Each rib was made of several solid sections of wood mortise-and-tenoned together. Near the outer edge where the shape of the ark curved sharply upward, Japheth had placed specially ordered beams cut from naturally bent or leaning trees. This added great strength to the structure. The sectional ribs connected by mortise and tenon joints were slightly flexible and would allow the ark to flex without losing its integrity. This, Shem and Noah thought, would be something important for such a large, heavily-loaded craft in deep and turbulent waters.

As each rib was attached, two layers of outside planks were added, which would be the actual hull of the ark, against which the waves of the flood waters would pound. These were carefully overlapped, fit tightly into place, caulked with pine pitch and wool, and held into place by iron spikes forged with a square head on the outside and bent over on the inside. Then, as each row of hull boards went on, a protective coat of dark colored pitch was brushed on to protect the wood and iron from moisture and insects.

Many of the outside planks needed to be bent to form a better and stronger hull. This was done according to the advice from the sea captain befriended by Shem and Noah. A board to be bent was laid over a pit of hot coals and rocks. The ends of the board rested on flat stones at the edge of the pit. Something of great weight was placed at the center of the board. When the coals had heated the rocks, water was

79

poured into the pit and all was covered to trap the heat and steam. After several hours, the softened plank would sag and be allowed to bend to the desired degree, then allowed to cool. Several inches of permanent bend could be achieved this way making it much easier to create a smooth and very resilient outer surface of the ark.

The process of adding rib sections and siding continued slowly. The huge, dark, pitch-colored object rose from the ground and became such a common sight in the compound that it lost some of its original mystery. There it was, a slow growing thing, day after day, year after year. Every day, except the seventh day of rest that Noah strictly enforced, beams or planks were added. As work progressed, some of the scaffolding that held the original shape could be removed as workers were able to move around inside the ark climbing like insects over the hulk hoisting, pounding and chiseling the thing into shape.

Finally, with the hull nearly done, it was time to put into place the three decks demanded in Noah's description received from God. When decks were in place it would be time to begin detailed preparations for the many kinds of passengers to be invited onboard.

18

Making Pitch

In a forest some miles from the compound there grew a particular kind of tree with evergreen needles. Ages before Noah's time, men found that these trees, when wounded, oozed an amber-colored, sticky substance which people of the land used almost on a daily basis. A wealthy merchant in town had strict control over the harvesting, processing and sale of this substance. He hired underlings, mostly young slaves captured in battle, to harvest this "pine pitch" for sale in the market. It was very much in demand. The merchant had fought off other interests and gained access to sections of the forest to which he sent his slaves each day to collect sap. With special blades, they wounded the trees and the stuff would ooze slowly into vessels made of bark. The boys were seen every day trudging barefoot along roadsides toward town, a pole bent over their shoulder with a goat skin of heavy pitch on each end.

The sap was heated, purified and sold in the marketplace in various forms. Most of it was traded to the group of suppliers assigned to the current ruler who commanded the army. He used the substance to water-seal fortifications, craft leather shields, affix spear and arrow points and to fill the cauldrons of flaming pitch made ready for the heads of enemies who were foolish enough to lay siege to his city wall.

When mixed with tallow, made from rendered animal fat, pine sap made a fresh smelling soap to clean skin or clothing. The women kept a supply of it in every home. In its thin, clear form it worked as fuel in lamps, but it burned very hot and didn't last as long as a good animal or nut oil. It had healing properties when used to seal a cut on the flesh. When mixed with black charcoal powder it burned hot and bright on the end of a torch. Laborers nearly always carried a few bits of pitch in their pouch for wounds or for starting a fire. Everyone was taught from childhood to be careful with pitch. It was annoyingly sticky on hands and if a lump caught fire the sticky flame was a dangerous thing.

Most importantly for Noah's project, pitch was both a glue and a sealer, so it was useful for holding water in or holding water out. Rivermen knew this. They had used it to seal their wooden barges for many years. And, when mixed with sheep dung, a little bit of the costly material went a long way. Much experimenting was done, such as adding sheep's wool to add strength and flexibility.

This useful substance from trees was important in the culture, but especially to Noah's family, because God had specified that the gigantic ark be coated inside and out with pitch, so they were going to need a lot of it. This increased demand caused the price of pitch to rise in the market and was an additional source of conflict with people of the city.

19

Lamech's Visit

Sentries near the wall were the first to hear the faint sound of trumpet blasts echoing from the distant forest. A flock of crows rose from a field in the direction of the sound and circled over the compound. Noah, his sons, their wives and all but a very few of the servants and workers knew what this meant. They quickly dressed in clean linen, came from their places and gathered in columns by the main gate. Additional sentries, dressed in dark red ceremonial tunics, pale red turbans with the distinctive gold cord, stood at regular intervals along each side of the road outside the gate. Then Noah, walking with a golden staff, stood in the entrance of the compound while four of the red sentries raised ram's horns to their lips and answered the distant trumpets with seven blasts of their own.

Two runners came over the crest of the hill, slowly approached the party of sentries, took off their headgear, laid down their spears and bowed low before Noah, who quickly asked them to rise.

"Is my father with you my friend, and is he well?" Noah asked.

"Yes, my lord. Your father lives and has health and strength graciously given by the almighty Creator God who he serves."

Every few years, Noah's father, Lamech, traveled from his lands several day's distance to pay a personal visit and maintain the vital family connection so important to descendants of Adam's son, Seth. It had been many years since Lamech's father Methuselah had visited the compound. Enoch, Lamech's grandfather had been taken up by his God some four centuries prior to this time. Nevertheless, by means of a carefully kept oral tradition, Methuselah, Lamech, Noah and now the three sons, were able to know all that Enoch knew, all that had been revealed to him during his life-long walk with Creator God. Fathers taught their families as well as key servants these traditions and all were charged to devise ways to remember and recite. Most importantly, these truths were meant to produce in the community the wisdom that comes with reverence for God, the joy and contentment of fellowship with God, something lost in such large measure by Man's fall from grace.

And now, with Lamech coming, there was not only the welcome of family, but another chance to link to the past.

After a large gathering, including nearly everyone in the compound, with much food, music and fellowship, Noah gestured to his sons and their wives to join him and their grandfather at the center of the compound around the evening fire. Stools were set out. Servants fed the fire, prodded the coals, offered hot drinks and stood by with woolen blankets as the evening air grew cool. The sun had set leaving streaks of gold across the western sky.

Old Lamech, despite being well into his eighth century of life, moved without assistance and was in good spirits for having endured such a long, stressful day of travel and celebration. He was offered one of the padded, pine-log benches near the warm fire circle and sat listening attentively as Noah and the others updated him on the many affairs of the compound. They did their best to describe to him Noah's divine revelation, including the very disturbing word of God's desire to put an end to all people. This news was delivered very soberly and all those present were silent for some time. Then, Noah described the overwhelming challenges of building the ark, the unnerving certainty of the coming calamity and the very many frustrations they faced confronting the public with these realities.

Despite the shocking nature of the revelations, Lamech continued to listen calmly.

For Noah and the brothers, the time with grandfather was an emotional venting, a rare chance to open their painfully burdened hearts to someone who did not scoff or ridicule. They were prepared for him to call them crazy as others had done. But the old man, who they deeply loved and respected, was the first sympathetic ear they had encountered. As it would turn out, he would also be the last and only sympathetic ear.

"Let me tell you something that might encourage you," the old man said. "Or, at least, I might be able to dispel some of your fears and self-doubt. When God said to you that he was going to put an end to all people, for the world was filled with violence because of them, I would concur that he was speaking truth."

He held up his hands as if expecting dissent. "Yes, yes, I know God can speak only truth! But let me verify, from my own experience, that virtually all the people of the earth have, indeed, become corrupted in all their ways. The earth is, in truth, filled to overflowing with violence. I have lived nearly six centuries and have traveled far. You see it. I see it. We wonder how our good and just God can bear it, for we find it overwhelming. Your land, my land and all lands inhabited by descendants of Seth son of Adam, are filled with violence. It seems the will of Man is wounded unto death. No salve, no cure has been found. The wound festers and the smell of it has reached the heavens."

As he spoke a distant shout, that of a large crowd, rose from a mile away across the river in the direction of, what the city called, The Field of Public Gathering. Waves of cheering and shouting drifted over the compound for several moments. A faint orange glow could be seen near the horizon in that direction.

"It is the beginning of harvest," Ham explained apologetically. "Sacrifices are made there on the people's altar at sunset. Someone, perhaps more than one, has just now been offered to the gods."

They sat in silence until the cheering subsided.

"May I ask you something Grandfather? What did you mean when you said, 'The will of Man is wounded?'"

"It's the underlying reality each of us and future generations need to understand," Lamech answered. "Adam, in his refusal to deny himself in his search for pleasure, saw what pleased him, reached out and took it as Eve had done.

86

He took what was forbidden and brought about his expulsion from Paradise."

"As we know, and the world refuses to acknowledge, that willful, disobedient act of the first man has brought a self-inflicted wound upon the will of all men, a will meant to rest in the abundance and sufficiency of God himself. Cursed is the ground because of Adam's choice and corrupted is the will of all men. And since Adam, no human being, male or female, has found contentment, except those who rest in the sufficiency of God."

The old man looked straight at Ham, "All this is foolishness to the wise of this world! Isn't it Ham?" The old man's eyes widened. "Why would a man deny himself pleasure? How could fasting bring life? How could dependency on an invisible God be anything but subserviency? Are we not free to look after ourselves?"

Then the old man leaned forward, tapped Ham on the knee, and said, "The will of man is wounded and twisted. It seeks pleasure and gets only pain. It is chronically bent toward self-gratification. Eve first, then Adam, then the whole of humanity slid down the muddy bank of desire into the river of sin and were swept away into death."

"But there is a way that leads to life. Few find it, but it is the path of righteousness. Listen not to the deceiving serpent! He crouches at your door. Keep your thoughts and actions in line with the commands of the Lord God. Follow his ways. Deny the lusts of the flesh and depend fully on his provision, for he is good and will not, cannot fail you!"

These were heavy words. All listening reflected on their own ways as their hearts were stirred.

87

Shem asked quietly, "Is this what they mean when they say, 'Enoch walked with God?'"

"Yes, it is the way in which Enoch walked and I have desired to walk."

Then he leaned over and put his hand on the knee of Noah, and said proudly, "And from all I hear, it is the way of Noah."

Japheth asked, "How does one begin to walk in this way?"

"It is to acknowledge your identity with Adam. That is the beginning. And it is something we all forget." Lamech answered, "It goes against our flesh to accept that we are blind, naked and dumb without the fellowship and divine guidance of the Lord God himself."

Lamech bowed his head and said, as if speaking to himself, "Oh, how I long to walk with him in the cool of the morning as they did in the early days of Paradise. Only in a close walk with him can I ever find the strength and grace to be able to withdraw my hands from the pleasures of this world, denying myself fruit that can only bring death, and wait upon God, wait for as long as it takes, for fruit from the tree that gives life."

Lamech looked up and went on in a brighter tone, "Now here's the really good news. We can look forward to the fulfillment of God's first promise. Do you remember what that first promise was?" he asked the group.

Shem said, "That the seed of the woman would crush the serpent's head and he would bruise his heel."

"Yes," Lamech said, "that deceiving serpent the devil. For all these centuries we have looked for the fulfillment of those mysterious words. We believe God will make things right. He will provide a way to escape the evils of sin and death. As you build the ark, remember that God takes care of those who acknowledge him, keep his commands and bow to his authority. This ark, though we cannot comprehend it now, may represent this seed. It may be a shadow of what is to come. Or, rather, I should say *who* is to come, a champion, a mighty warrior, who will fight for us, do for us what we cannot do for ourselves, restore our wounded wills and set things right."

Noah turned toward his father and spoke. "I trust in God and will obey what he has asked us to do. And I know that he, the wise God of Creation, must have his reasons for destroying mankind and the earth. But I have difficulty, if I am being honest, to balance his justice with his goodness. How could such a good and wise God bring calamity upon his own creation?"

Lamech thought for a moment, then stood behind Noah and rested his hands on Noah's shoulders.

"I am no wiser than you, my son, and no more able to fathom the thoughts of the Lord God than you. I believe you ask, not because you doubt the justice of God, but because of the great weight of the call of God upon you. It is beyond your understanding. It is beyond all understanding. Still, we must have an answer for those who ask, if only to quiet the fears of our own hearts.

"This is what I would say. First of all, God is good. He created us because of the goodness of his heart and his desire to share his goodness. All goodness finds its source in him. Indeed, if God were anything other than good, we could not think rightly about anything. We could not rightly divide right from wrong, good from evil. How could we? There would be no basis for belief. The bedrock of belief is God's goodness.

"And God is just. Do not we, ourselves, creatures made in his image desire to see moral equity prevail in all human society. That longing, that desire for justice, which is at the basis of all human interaction, can only come from our Creator's own perfect justice. He is unchangeably just and no respecter of persons. We leave vengeance to him for this reason. His goodness and justice are in perfect harmony and we can cast our doubts and fears aside and trust him fully. A good God will be just and a just God will be good."

At this, the old man clapped his hands, lifted up his head and laughed at himself, startling the group.

"Easy for me to say!" he exclaimed. "I am not the one who must build a monstrous sea-going vessel where there is no sea and explain myself to scoffers! Noah, *you* have been given that unenviable task! Lord God have mercy!"

And he had a good laugh at Noah's expense and the small group burdened with so many cares and worries tried their best to laugh along.

They visited around the fire for some time until all were ready to retire to their dwellings.

As they rose from their places Lamech took a step toward Noah, looked directly at him and said, "My son, I have watched you grow and accomplish many things. Now, you are working on a task larger than any man has imagined or attempted. You will always be remembered for your obedience to God in the building of this ark. I am most proud of your faith. Against resistance and persecution you have not wavered in your walk. Among peoples of my land and far beyond, you are known as that crazy man that still believes in the Creator God. But I know you are not crazy."

Everyone standing there by the fire chuckled nervously.

Lamech continued, "Noah, faithless fools may scoff at you, but you have walked with God and have certainly exceeded me and all others in faith and wisdom. You have heard God's voice and you have obeyed. That is wisdom itself! God bless you for that!"

Lamech then, with one hand on Noah's shoulder and the other lifted to the night sky, said, "Now, may his everlasting presence be your reward. May his wisdom, power and grace be your sufficiency. And may he provide abundantly all that you need to fulfill the exceedingly challenging calling upon your life."

In that moment, an unseen burden of anxiety, fear and doubt lifted from all their hearts as there was a crackling in the fire and a host of sparks rose to mingle in the stars.

Did you know? - *According to biblical genealogical accounts, Lamech lived to be 777 and died just five years before the flood. Methuselah, whose name means "sending forth" died at age 969 the same year as the flood. Some believe his name refers to the flood which was sent on the same year as his death.*

20

Dealing with Doubt

The three brothers didn't get much time for leisure except on the weekly day of rest, a tradition long ago established by forefathers in the line of Seth. On one such day they had a rare opportunity to leave the wives at home, sit and converse together under a large oak at the far edge of the building field. There was a very pleasing view of the meadow, the pond and the rolling hills of their father's orchards which extended off to the west. Animal sounds arose from the woods nearby and a flock of ducks feeding in the bullrushes began making a racket as the morning mist was dispelled by rays of the sun.

There was a soft fluttering in the branches of a bush near them where four or five tiny sparrows leapt from branch to branch picking at invisible things sending a whirring vibration through the morning air. Ham was the first to notice it and dropped out of their conversation to watch the little innocent creatures do what he knew birds did so amazingly well. In that confined bramble of twisted branches the little acrobats went about their business of being birds without any care except to enjoy doing what they were made to do.

"They don't know what is coming do they? What must it be like to be without a care?" Ham asked of no one in particular. "I hate to see the innocent creatures go."

The three remained sitting there watching the birds for a long silent moment until the birds left, called away by some soft, unseen voice, one by one, they disappeared into the woods as wonderfully as they had appeared.

Months of mind-bending stress and nearly unbearable responsibility had left the brothers with little emotional capacity to stop and let the reality sink in, to grieve for the effect the coming destruction would have on the natural world around them. Their thoughts had been of humanity, the thousands upon thousands of souls that inhabited the land, many of whom were their own relatives, workmates and boyhood friends. But here too, was this beautiful, magical world of little birds, and the whole, vibrant realm of living, breathing creatures they represented. They had contributed nothing to the corruption of mankind, but would be tragic victims of the judgement that was to come. Those little winged beings, free as they seemed, probably had their own struggles being affected deeply by what had been brought upon all creation through the fall of Man. Their Creator, these men knew, cared for those sparrows, each one. He had feathered them and implanted their rapidly beating little hearts with a purpose in mind. When he set them to flight, he looked upon them and saw that they were good. He loved them as he did all creation.

In that moment the crushing weight of it all fell upon the hearts of Noah's sons. The awfulness of God's judgement. Nature's frailty before an almighty God. The unwillingness of humanity to change, to avoid what was to come. The sad burden of it settled on them and they walked to their homes unable to inwardly grasp with their minds what the Creator must be contemplating in his infinite wisdom. It was too much to comprehend. To be honest, they didn't want any of it.

It would have been easy for them to be dislodged in that moment from their commitment to the work their father's family had been called to. They could have lost faith or thrown it off. But, they chose to hang on, by some ingrained strength, to what they called their "anchor." They understood what an anchor was, a strong stake driven into firm ground to which lines were attached. Knowledge of the Creator was this stabilizing anchor of faith to which their sense of resolve was attached. It kept their souls. Its lines ran back to the beginning.

They knew, from what they had been told, God was truly wise. He could see the end from the beginning. And they had begun to understand what wisdom was, at least in part. Wisdom, they had been taught, was the ability to devise perfect ends and achieve those ends by perfect means, something only God could do. So, by this firm tradition, they believed they could rest in their Creator who was infinitely wise, and in his words passed on by forefathers, believing their Lord God was both all-knowing and all- powerful. They had heard, since early childhood, of this God and of the conflict that raged in the earth between the wisdom of God and the cunning trickery of the serpent spirit. Treachery and violence, the way of the cursed line of Cain, had spread across the land and now, the all-wise Creator God, in righteous judgement, was about to act against it.

At numerous times when their family had faced severe testing and persecution, they had seen their father raise his hands, even in the face of an angry crowd and say, with complete disregard for what the crowd might think, "Oh Lord my God, you made the heavens and the earth. You have made known your ways to the forefathers. And you sit upon the throne in heaven and your kingdom rules over all."

Noah's bold declarations caused everyone to take a step back. His outspoken faith in the face of danger demonstrated a courage his sons lacked. But it was a reassurance to the three that God in his wisdom had things under control when everything seemed out of control. They had heard Noah say, "Oh Lord, how many are your works. In wisdom you have made them all and we see your beauty in all you have made." The three knew that their father had a way of seeing what the people of the land had no interest in looking for. They desired to be as constant and fearless as their father in expressing what he believed.

But, they couldn't shake off the sadness of it all. They mourned for the earth. It was hard for them to maintain their trust and pour themselves fully into the work they were called to do. It was tradition and their father's spiritual strength that kept them going.

21

The Mob at Night

Work progressed slowly as the years passed. The massive keel was in place, the ribs attached and hundreds of overlapping planks began to form a boat-like shape. Japheth's crews were encouraged to see it rise from the earth as each new row of planks was added.

It was in about the fiftieth year of the project when, late one evening, sentries at the front gate of the compound came knocking on Japheth's door. Something was happening near the bridge leading to the compound. Japheth got dressed, roused several of his servants and ran to the gate to see what was the matter.

Across the river a procession of men with lit torches was moving out from the open gate of the city, across the bridge and onto the road leading to the compound. Behind the large brigade of torch bearers there came a long line of men. From the light of the torches, Japheth could see the reflection of many spear heads and other metal blades of various sorts. By the disorderly way they were coming, it didn't appear to be the militia sent and led by official command. This appeared to be the men of the town coming to pay Noah an unfriendly visit.

As progress had been made on the ark, especially after it became visible over the walls of the compound, word had spread that the ark's mysterious presence was casting some kind of bad omen onto the city. Something had provoked a sudden panic and that night the men of the city decided to put an end to this ark and to Noah as well.

By the time the torch bearers reached the front gate, Shem and Ham had arrived with their wives.

A leader of the mob, carrying a spear, was let in who angrily told the brothers that the ark had to be destroyed that same night and there was going to be no discussion.

Red in the face he said, "Noah's fiasco is over! It is time for this insanity to end! The town is tired of the old senile fool stealing all the labor and materials to build this monstrous, evil object that threatens to bring calamity on us all! We know of your evil motives! Tonight it burns!"

The leader's demeanor softened a bit when he noticed Noah pushing his way up to face him.

Ham abruptly stepped into the space between the leader and Noah, grabbed hold of the shaft of the leader's spear and the two men stood chest to chest glaring at each other for a long moment. Noah, not having time to fully dress, stood there bare-headed in his simple linen night garment, the only white-haired one in the crowd.

"No one is going to burn anything tonight," Ham said to the leader's face.

Noah was about to speak when the gate was pushed open and a hundred men with torches stormed past the leader with a shout pushing Noah's family and servants to the side. The brothers grabbed Noah's arms escorting him out of harm's way as the crowd rushed toward the building field. Japheth yelled to his wife to bring all the servants and wives at once to the stone security house and to remain there. He, Shem and Ham moved with Noah along the edge of the crowd toward the field.

The light of the torches lit the long, rounded hull of the great vessel. It was an eerie object in that light, its uncovered ribs pointing upward looking like the skeletal remains of some giant creature. The men with torches had gathered in one group near the edge of the pit in which the ark lay. They were pausing for a confused moment, waiting for some kind of command from their leaders.

Noah, guarded by his sons, moved slowly through the crowd to where the torch men stood. He stepped up onto a small pile of wooden beams and in the torch light could be seen by all.

Many years later, Shem would tell others this was the proudest moment of his life, seeing his father standing there in a simple white gown on that dark night of terror, facing the mob without a trace of fear.

Noah said in a clear, sharp voice, "You come against us with spears and fire. I am here to tell you that you had better think twice about the wicked thing you have conspired to do. I am but an old man with my three sons, our wives and a few servants. What are we against so many? But listen to me now. Put your anger and fear aside. Put your spears and torches down if you want to return to your homes alive. The Lord God has told me to build this ark and it will be built. I'd advise you go the way you came and no harm will come to you tonight. It is a fearful thing to fall into the hands of the Lord God who created the heavens and the earth. I say to you, we serve the Living God, and no spear can stop what he has planned. And no torch can burn what he has begun. At this moment, you stand as between a bear and her cubs. Go now. Cross the bridge to the safety of your homes, while you can."

The men with torches looked from Noah to each other, then to their leader who seemed to be without an answer. One could see that Noah's words had had an effect. They had come to rid themselves of some bad omen, but now they hesitated. They knew Noah was not a small, trivial man. He had always been a man of honor and of good reputation. And his words that evening were spoken with a fearful kind of authoritative power.

Their leader pushed himself to the center of the crowd where Noah stood. But he said nothing. Ham, as before, moved forward to defend his father. But Noah said to Ham, "We needn't fear him Ham. He is finished here."

Then Noah shouted over the crowd, "You are finished here!"

When he said those words, the leader fell back against the first rank of torch bearers and there was confusion among them. The torches, which had been burning for some time, began to flicker and go out, one by one. Then, starting from the rear of the crowd, men began to murmur and move back along the edge of the pit toward the gate and as quickly as they had come, the visitors from the city were gone.

22

Noah Preaches

The night of the angry crowd with torches was not the first time the ark project was threatened and it wouldn't be the last, but it was the closest rioters had come to actually setting fire to and destroying the work God had asked Noah to do.

When Noah's wife returned home from the stone safety house that night, she was furious.

"They had spears this time, didn't they Noah?" she said, "They could have killed you! What then? They would have taken the compound and all of us would have been enslaved or banished. What then?"

Noah was tired and shaken by the events of the evening. He sat on the edge of the bed next to Nayiri. "You're right," he said, "it was a frightening thing and I was afraid for you and the others. But when they stopped at the pit and waited for their leader, I knew they wouldn't do it. They couldn't do it. I'm sorry to put you through that, but I knew the Lord God would not allow it."

She stood and looked at him. "He would not allow it? Did you think he would send angels? Would he cause the wood not to burn? And you! Out there in your bed clothes looking like a fool! Do you think you could have stopped that mob?"

"No. But this is not my project to save. It is God's project. And he would have to save it. I am so certain that this is the will of God, that there is no way he would have allowed an unruly mob to thwart his plans. It just wouldn't. . . . it just couldn't happen!"

"You got lucky."

"No, not lucky. God put their torches out."

Nayiri thought about that for a moment, then asked, "Well, what are you going to do now?"

"I am going to speak to the officials and city leaders." Noah answered. "They need to hear again what this ark represents and what the Lord God is about to do. A mob coming with torches to destroy the ark tells me they still do not understand what I've been preaching all these years. I will get the sons to arrange a meeting."

The next day, Shem, Japheth and Ham spread the word in the city that Noah would be presenting his case before all who would listen. There would be a gathering at the front gate of the compound and all were encouraged to come.

On the appointed day, officials, leaders, rivermen, merchants, towns folks and trouble makers all crossed the bridge and formed a large crowd outside Noah's gate. The officials in formal attire stood at the front with their security guards. They glared at Noah as he ascended the small wooden platform built into the "safe space" at the side of the gate. People were used to seeing him there. He had been preaching and teaching from that place each full moon for decades.

After Japheth had quieted the crowd, Noah thanked them for coming, as loud as he could, louder than he usually had to, for this crowd was bigger than most.

Someone from the crowd yelled, "Noah, you're a madman!"

"My friends," Noah responded, "I assure you that I am not mad, unless one calls doing the will of God madness. I am doing what the God of Adam, Seth and Enoch has commanded. Most of you know of this God, but like Adam, you have chosen to turn your back on him."

"We have our own gods!" someone yelled.

"Yes. Tiny bronze gods you can carry in your pocket! Let me tell you about the God I serve.

"He is the God of our fathers and he is calling all people to himself for the healing of their souls. He has been calling all men everywhere ever since the mother and father of all mankind sinned against him by transgressing a simple command given to them.

"In the beginning, when the world was new, God communed with Adam and Eve in the garden we call Eden. He repeatedly declared his love for them and demonstrated that love by giving them many things to enjoy: fruits and other foods that were delicious beyond description, animal companions of every sort, flowers, trees, as well as the entire world. Creation possessed a radiant beauty that was a delight to their eyes. Truly, they lived in an earthly paradise. And the most precious times of each day were those quiet hours when they would walk and talk with their Creator. God intended that they mature in relationship to him and fulfill the initial image they had received, being made in the very image of God. By God's help and through their obedience, they could attain the full likeness of God in wisdom, goodness and righteousness, learning from him what is good and what is evil."

One of the officials raised his hand and stepped forward.

"We know that story! We've heard you before Noah. But it is old tales from the land of shadows. What do old myths have to do with us?" he asked loudly. The crowd murmured in agreement.

"There is a difference, my friend, between a myth and a mystery," Noah answered, quieting the crowd with both hands. "You may *want* this to be myth, so as not to be morally responsible. But it is history passed to us by righteous forefathers. And, admittedly, much of it is mystery. But we are not left in the dark.

"First, I want to remind you of the nature of sin that entered the world through disobedience.

"Because of their willful disobedience to and defiance of God's will, Eve and Adam severed their life-giving relationship with God. They did this when they began pursuing their own desires, having been deceived by the serpent, the hater of God and of all who bear God's image. Since there is no life apart from God, death came to Eve and Adam. God had told them, if they eat of the forbidden tree they would certainly die. Sin entered their hearts. The result of sin is death, first spiritual, then physical.

"But listen to me. The Lord God has provided a solution.

"Adam and Eve knew they had sinned and were filled with shame. And God knew. And while they were sinners, he sought them in the garden to restore them to himself. And that same God wants to restore you and me, all sinners before him, to himself.

"You are all well aware of the effects of sin in our world. The violence and death. Every heart is set against knowledge of God and his ways. Every thought is of wicked intentions."

Another one shouted from the crowd. "Enough about all that! We've heard this before. We're all sinners. Yeah. Yeah. We know. But what about this ark of yours?"

"Because of sin and the depth of that sin, God is bringing judgment upon this world," Noah went on. "He is going to unleash a great flood that will destroy all flesh except those animals and those people who will take refuge in this ark that we are building. The end of this present age is surely coming soon. God is calling you to turn and to trust him for the healing of your souls and so that you may find refuge from the flood in this ark."

Another man shouted, "What do you mean, *turn*?"

"Turn from your own ways and walk in his ways," Noah said. "Believe him. Trust him."

The official asked, "I agree with you Noah, that this world is a mess. I even agree with you about Adam and Eve, sin and death. But we have religion to take care of that. My problem is, that this is the way things have always been and will always be. Nothing has changed. The world just keeps on going, season after season, year after year. And that's the way it will always be! So, preach if you want, but stop this talk about a coming catastrophe. *It's not going to happen!*"

Then the official turned to the crowd and asked, "Do any of you see a flood coming?"

The crowd yelled, "No!"

"Do any of you feel the earth shake?"

"No!"

"So, I suggest to you old man," he said turning to Noah, "that you go on with your little project, but leave predictions about the weather to our holy men!"

With that, the crowd roared with laughter.

Noah shouted over the laughter, "God's promises are sure! The Flood is coming! But remember, God loves you and does not desire that any perish. His words for you today are, 'Come unto me. I will forgive you and heal you.' Come to him today! Come any day! You are welcome here. This ark is your refuge."

Ripples of laughter emanated from the crowd as it slowly turned and retreated over the bridge.

23

Finishing the Ark

Slowly, very slowly, the ark had taken shape. Hundreds of barge loads of planks and beams had been hewn, shaped, bent, chiseled and pounded into place. Thousands of wrought-iron spikes, rivets and straps held parts in place. Miles of hemp rope woven by the women of the compound bound beams together. What seemed like an eternity of back-breaking work had produced something that was very close to what Shem and Noah had envisioned.

Over the decades since Noah first received the word from God, the great vessel rose inch by inch from what was once a bare, stony field. It was now the dark shape of something ominous, and at the same time, something rather pleasing to the eye as the final, exterior details were added. Its intended function had dictated its form. The fortitude and discipline of Noah and his sons had produced something of quality which, if one was to look closely at any particular part, he would find very little to complain about. Every plank in the hull had been tightly fit and the pitch and wool chinking between every board had been pounded tightly in place by a team of men under Japheth's direction.

It was exciting for the entire crew to begin the final phases of construction.

Now, the interior decking, partitions, walkways, staircases, storage, living quarters and such needed to be planned and built in. Some of the decking had been installed to provide access to the hull, but now they needed to be filled in and reinforced. This would take all the wood-fitting skill they had, for this interior space would need to hold and keep separate many, many creatures of many kinds. At this point, Noah didn't precisely know just which or how many animals would come, for they had not yet been sent. He could only estimate based on knowledge of the animal kingdom passed down to him from forefathers. Adam had, after all, named every one and had passed these names, as well as particulars, on to succeeding generations down to Noah.

And there were those giant reptiles to consider. Caravan captains and traders from the far east and the south had told of these legendary monsters, tall as trees with legs like pillars. Japheth's wife, Anahit, had bought a tooth of one of these giants at the market place and it now sat, carved into an oil lamp, on the table in their home.

They were part of the animal world and would have to be saved. But how? Was it possible?

Planning these challenges kept him and Shem up many evenings making lists, solving problems and building a theoretical inventory. Japheth and his wife had the basic knowledge to plan out the three decks, the partitions, cages, pens, perches, feeding troughs, waste shoots, water tanks and so on.

The Ark Being Constructed

Anahit insisted that there be comfortable living quarters for people passengers. At this point no one knew how many persons would be in the ark. Noah was optimistic that some people of the city would take to heart what he had been telling them and that they would come and join them. But, at the moment, even after a hundred years of preaching, none had responded with anything but laughter and ridicule.

Japheth, following Shem's advice, placed the human living quarters near the top of the vessel where it was thought that they would have best access to air and light. They did not know if the coming flood would be a calm rising or wickedly raging sea. Preparing for the worst, they thought there was a measure of safety to place the people at the top center surrounded by beasts. So, a sturdy room was built with space for each family. Walkways and staircases allowed access to all parts of the ark from deep in the belly, where they expected to house the heavy elephants, rhinos and such, up to the top where small animals and birds would be kept close to the screened windows built into the eighteen inch gap between the top deck and the roof.

A large, very sturdy door frame was constructed in the side at a height above the expected water line and accessible from the ground by a ramp made of earth shored up with heavy beams. This ramp which would be the means to take onboard two and four-legged creatures of all sorts, was also the entry point of the dozens of daily workers that built the interior of the ark.

Very much thought went into preparations for the animals, mostly under the direction of Anahit. Tight wooden cisterns were positioned along each side to collect rainwater and were connected by goat-skin tubes to suspended clay jars. By this system they could transfer water to each section of the vessel. Troughs were built in to permit removal of waste. Bronze rings were fastened to beams in nearly every stall to fasten harnesses and hemp ropes. The interior walls, beams and posts were white-washed with lime wash to reflect the little bit of light that would enter from the windows above and to provide sterile surfaces easier to clean. Special swinging oil lamps were hung along the passageways in the lower deck where light would be scarce. And special care was taken to keep openings for air flow, a problem Noah took very seriously. They were all used to animal smells, but this was going to be an extreme challenge.

He often said, "It is going to get very ripe in here!"

This work and the attachment of the large, flat roof took the final years of the project.

24

Noah's Prayer

During those days, anxious thoughts filled the minds of Noah's sons, their wives and the servants who could readily sense the tension in the air. As the looming shape of the ark grew at the edge of the compound even blocking out the sun near the end of every day, its shadow seemed to send a chill into everyone's heart. Rather than representing a great object of hope, it was becoming a symbol of coming disaster.

They knew, at least the immediate family understood, that the Lord God had given his word to save them and give them a new beginning and somehow, though devastation would come upon the earth and all life with breath be destroyed, they had a solid covenant with the Creator God himself, that they would be delivered. This was very clear from what Noah had told them. This ark, the very thing that had brought so much pain and misery for so long a time, was their means of deliverance.

But fears remained.

How would the devastation begin? From where could such waters come? How could they endure being surrounded by terror, death and destruction? And what would be the end? Would there be life at the end? It all seemed too impossible.

Noah, was tempted like all men. The continual stress brought him often to the breaking point. He had to take rests away from the work, just to refresh has weary old body and mind.

Fear would come upon him suddenly, without good reason, especially when he was physically spent. When his mind was overcome by doubt, he suffered pains of guilt and at times began to second-guess himself. But, strength of spirit tended to overcome the deception of flesh and he did what was his habit to do. He went for a walk with God and hashed it out.

At his bench under the pines, he knelt and pleaded. With his head on the ground, he listened desperately for the voice, the comfort, the reassurance of the Lord God. But, for many minutes he heard only the wind whispering in the pines. He waited. He tried to pray. He tried to worship. He brought to mind words of his forefathers concerning the goodness and mercy of God. He put his mind on what he knew to be true and fought to quiet the whispering voices of fear.

But, on one particularly bleak day, the still small voice he desired to hear, remained silent.

Frustrated, he stood to his feet, raised his hands and cried out, he lamented.

"Oh God, hear my cry!
You have been our dwelling place throughout all
generations.
Before these lands existed, you brought forth the earth

112

and placed Man here to serve you.
We sprout up like green grass in the morning,
and by evening we are dry and withered.
But you, oh Lord, are forever!
The senseless fools of this age do not know,
the wicked of this world do not understand.
Though they flourish today, they will not live to see your
glory.
In you the righteous will live and thrive.
They will grow like the mighty pine and sing in the wind
of your spirit.
My Lord, you have chosen me among all men and given
me favor.
Now, though the world fall away under me, I put my
trust in you.
For you are the vessel in whom I take refuge.
Though anxiety is great within me,
your consolation brings joy to my soul.
You are mightier than the thunder of great waters
and mightier than breakers of the sea.
Though you be silent, oh Lord,
your promises are sure and we put our trust in you."

25

Facing the Officials

Far to the west of Noah's lands the crust of the earth began to move. Weather patterns changed affecting the harvest of crops across the land.

A sense of foreboding spread through the city. Never, during the lifetime of all those living, and many had lived eight-hundred years or more, had anyone experienced such prolonged drought, such disturbing movements of the earth, darkening of the sky and dimming of the stars. Fear of these things had caused the Alya, holy men, mediums and sorcerers to be busier, and wealthier, than usual. There were many more shoes scattered outside the doors of temples as increased numbers of inquirers came to consult priests and offer prayers and sacrifices to the various gods. Failure of crops and a general dysfunction of commerce had stressed everyone in every walk of life. Thieves and looters were emboldened as order broke down and it became more dangerous than ever to risk being alone. Wagon loads of goods enroute to market, began to disappear. Families stayed in their houses and began to hoard food, which put everything in short supply.

It was a time of unraveling.

The rumor that these troubles were all having to do with Noah's ark spread again among the people and became a subject of discussion among city officials.

"This monstrous object in Noah's compound has disturbed the order of things, my lord!" an advisor said to the chief ruler at the council of nobles. "Some years back, when we sent people to torch that abominable thing, they became afraid and did not do what we asked them to do. Do they fear this Noah more than us? My lord, let us bring the old man before the council. We will deal with him!"

Word was sent.

Noah gathered his family.

"We knew something like this was going to happen," he said to them. "We've readied ourselves for this. It has never been socially acceptable to do the Lord's work. We are participants in a battle between the real kingdom of the Lord God, Creator of heaven and earth, and a false kingdom under the influence of the serpent who has set up a false rule among those who are sons of disobedience. But do not forget, my dear family, the realm of the serpent with all his evil cohorts, would not fit under a blade of grass in the kingdom of the Most High God!"

Noah clenched his fist and shook it. "Never forget who you are! We are created in his image! We belong to him and he will take us under his wings and keep us! We bow to no ruler, no noble. For our God is our refuge and our strength! He has commanded us and we will obey."

The family was silent for a long moment, then Shem stepped forward, put his arm around his father's shoulders and said, "We agree."

Then, one by one, Japheth, Ham and their wives moved forward to lay their hands onto Noah saying, "We agree. We agree."

Shem began to pray. His voice was so broken and full of emotion no one could quite understand what he said. His face was down and his voice muffled in the folds of his father's garments. Though they could not hear the words, they all felt the power and faith poured out. A sense of God's great love and grace was on them. They felt it. It was real. The love and unity of that moment was so unique in all their lives, so profound, that the fears that had been there just moments before, were cast out and the power and threats of city rulers and nobles seemed to lose all their force.

At the appointed time, Noah appeared with Shem before the ruling council.

"We have lost our patience, Noah," the chief ruler began. The group of advisors and religious leaders seated next to him on a raised platform nodded their heads in agreement.

"It is time for you to admit," he went on, "that this ark and the 'destruction of mankind,' as you put it, is the tall tale of mad man. It has disrupted our city by unnecessarily planting seeds of fear into the hearts of ignorant people. We, therefore, command you to dismantle what you have built. Or, we will take care of that for you. Do you understand?"

Noah stood with Shem, both of them with their pale red turbans in his hands, on a large red and gold carpet before steps leading up to the platform. Standing off to the side, there was a group of town elders, merchant leaders, Narek, commander of the river and older militia captains. Noah glanced around at everyone, then fixed his eyes on the city

116

ruler who sat before him in a large, ornate wooden chair at the center of the platform.

"I understand your intentions, my lord," Noah answered. "But, may I remind the council that my sons and I built this platform upon which you are now sitting. My son Shem, in fact, who stands here with me, carved into the ruler's official chair the lion's claws at its feet, the rising sun behind the ruler's head and the leaves and vines upon which our ruler's hands now rest."

The ruler lifted his hands, looked at the arm rests of the chair and smiled.

"I did not know that," he said, amused. Then looking around at the others, "We are appreciative of your fine work, Noah. But, what does that have to do with the subject before us?"

"That work, my lord, represents the many years I have been a servant of this city and the many contributions I have made in many ways to your people. Since long before you ruled here, my gate has been open to all who have come for help, healing, counsel or encouragement. There is not one among you who can bring a legitimate charge against me or my family. Rather, nearly everyone in this room has profited from my presence in this community as a grower of food, builder of needed things and helper to those who have become lost in this sinful world. So, I ask you sir, if a spring brings forth fresh water for generations, blessing all who draw from it, how can it be accused of being an offense against those whom it has refreshed?"

"Can anyone here verify what this man is saying?" the ruler asked sternly, looking around the room.

117

Hesitatingly, an older merchant stepped forward. "We must admit, my lord, that Noah's workers did, indeed, design and build this room, and that during the past years of drought, Noah's crops did not fail as others did. Somehow, he has been able to continue delivering fruits, vegetables and grains to market, which have kept us in business and our people from, well, sir. . . disaster."

"But what about this ark?" the ruler asked annoyed. No one responded.

Then, he looked angrily down at Shem, "You! Son of Noah! You do not look like a fool. You look like a sensible man! Tell us, do you really, deep down, believe what your father has been preaching? Is this ark, this sea-going monstrosity built on dry land, going to save us from some kind of catastrophic deluge sent from God because we are all bad people? What kind of God would do that? Do you believe this God who has spoken such evil things?"

The ruler's face turned increasingly red as he vented his frustration. He threw up his hands and turned away, not expecting an answer from the son.

But Shem stepped forward and gave an answer.

"My dear ruler and esteemed council members, I cannot speak for my father, but only from what I have witnessed. Yes, I believe what my father says, because I believe the Creator God has spoken to him."

"Ha! Does this God speak to you too?" demanded the ruler.

"You know as well as I, that in the beginning God created the heavens and the earth by the word of his mouth. Our

118

forefathers have made this clear. Is that not correct, dear ruler?"

"Yes. We are all aware of these myths."

"He spoke and it was done." Shem continued. "He commanded and from nothing came everything. He spoke to chaos and it became order. Even if you don't follow that tradition, the invisible reality of God, his power and deity, is clearly seen all around us in the things he has made. We are all without excuse."

"Oh, really?" the leader asked sarcastically.

"Yes. God speaks. He is not silent as a bronze idol. The voice of God is the most powerful force in nature, indeed, the *only* force. He speaks and the earth brings forth its wonders. The sun pours out its glory. The stars move in their assigned paths in the heavens. Our hearts beat within our chests. All is sustained by the living word of God. He is not silent! As he spoke at creation he speaks today. As he walked in the garden with Adam and Eve, he desires to walk with us today and speak to us. He wants to be heard. But we close our ears! Why? Because of our preoccupation with sin and self. We are too busy worshipping ourselves, or deaf and dumb bronze idols!"

The religious leaders on the platform, stirred in their seats, gathered up their robes and grumbled.

Shem went on, "Each day, dear ruler, the dew waters our lands. Do you see it?"

"Yes. So what?"

"The word of God is like that dew. It distills unto our hearts and stirs our conscience. His thoughts cover us as the dew covers the earth. He wishes to dwell with us and speak to our hearts. All of this is too wonderful, too awesome for any mind to understand. But when we open our hearts to God, he shows us what is right."

One of the religious leaders spoke up, "What is right young man?" Then he looked around at the others for assurance that he had, indeed, asked a clever question.

"Did not God speak to your father, Cain, and ask, 'Why is your face downcast? If you do what is right, will you not be accepted?"

"Yes. If you believe that ancient tradition!" the man answered, uncomfortable to be kin to Cain.

"I plead with you to search your own conscience. Follow the way that is right. Do not continue in the ways of Cain walking as sons of disobedience. Open your heart, as I have done, to determine if what my father says is true. I have come to know and trust the God of Noah's fathers. He is the God of Creation. He has revealed himself to us through what he has made and has spoken to my father about what is to come. Listen to him. I'm not sure you realize just how important it is that you do."

There was a general commotion in the room as the officials conferred together casting hostile glances at the two standing before them. The ruler adjourned the meeting and dismissed everyone without making it clear what was decided, if anything.

Noah and Shem, escorted by several servants, returned home without incident. Though not much was said along the way, Shem could see that his father was smiling.

"What are you thinking?" Shem asked him.

"I was thinking maybe it's time I turn the preaching over to you!" Noah said with a laugh.

On Shem's part, he was second-guessing himself, thinking of all the things he *could* have said, or *should* have said to the officials.

But, it was done, they had spoken, and now, as always, everything was in the hands of God.

26

Tremors Begin

There was a reason for the recent drought in the land. During the last few years of building the ark, seven to be exact, there were some serious disruptions in the normal pattern of life on the planet. The atmosphere was changing. And the ground began heaving. The ark itself got its first test against the elements as its timbers shook and swayed. The morning dew, so dependable, so important for all living things, began to dissipate earlier in the day leaving less condensation on the land than before. Plants withered. A kind of smokey haze replaced the crystal-clear blue sky everyone was used to. The sun turned slightly red and the moon a murky shade of orange. Sunsets and sunrises became frightening spectacles of color no one had seen. And the ground shook clay pots off everyone's shelves.

The merchant selling pots in the city was among the very few who prospered. Solid structures of mud and brick cracked and crumbled. At times, tremors were so severe, people slept in the streets for fear of having their buildings fall on them in the night. Even the great brick oven that had been at the center of the market for centuries collapsed in a cloud of dust.

But worst of all, the drought brought the first threats of famine in the land, something they were not prepared for.

Murmurings against Noah began again and would have broken out into violence but for the fact that Noah's crops, for strange reasons, seemed to be surviving the drought and he was one of the only suppliers able to keep food products coming to the market.

Visitors to Noah's "safe place" in the gate became so frequent it was hard for the family to provide the comfort and counsel needed.

"What's going on?" Ham asked his father.

"I can only wonder," Noah said, "if the catastrophe God talked about is beginning to come upon the earth. The signs are all around."

Indeed, at the far edge of a continent at the far edge of a sea, the earth was beginning to come apart.

Unknown to Noah and peoples of the land in which he lived, pressure was building between two large masses of the earth's crust. Since creation the earth had remained relatively quiet and done little to disturb the affairs of Man or beast. But, at an appointed time, some unseen hand touched the earth, upsetting the balance of things and setting into motion a chain of catastrophic events that would change everything.

The thin, fragile crust of the earth, floating paper-thin upon a vast, churning ball of fire, began to give way to the heat and pressure of the molten rock below. A delicate balance had been disturbed. Cubic miles of white-hot molten magma poured up through fissures in the crust spewing dust and gases into the atmosphere. As the earth spun on its axis and the winds wrapped around from west to east, the dust and debris from the volcanic eruptions covered the earth, dimming the sun, cooling the surface and disrupting life in Noah's world.

For seven years this cracking of the plates that make up the earth's crust continued, and increased steadily. The haze deepened. Plants, animals and people grew desperate. The daily patterns of the earth that had blessed and sustained life, began to break up.

People were not yet in a full state of panic, but they had lost their patience with the leaders and officials who reassured them over and again that this would all pass.

Only Noah and his family suspected that this was just the very beginning.

The distant convulsions that were causing weather to change and pots to break in Noah's land were minor inklings of a massive, cataclysmic event beyond anyone's comprehension that was about to reform the entire surface of the earth.

Did you know? -- *It may interest the reader to note that, many centuries after the deluge, petrified trees unearthed from sediment layers across the earth, very often show the final seven growth rings to be especially thin. This is very likely the result of seven years of drought just before having their bark stripped off and being buried swiftly beneath mud and rock.*

27

The Final Days

Noah's wife was the first to speak up about the fine dust that was settling on every surface in the house. The smoke and haze in the atmosphere had begun to settle in a noticeable way, like a fine ash. No one had seen anything like this before. It was beginning to annoy anyone trying to keep tables, shelves and work surfaces clean. And it was making people cough.

This disturbance in the earth's crust had begun years before on the other side of the planet and would intensify. The tremors in the ground became a daily occurrence. What could be shaken had already cracked and fallen. The market place had all but closed down as goods became scarce. Many occupants of the city had left for the delta, thinking that in the low country they could escape the shaking, the drought and the dust.

Noah, Japheth, Shem and Ham met to discuss their current situation. The ark was structurally finished, three decks, lower, middle and upper, covered by a roof, with spaces for all the various kinds of animals that they had knowledge of. Food supplies had been stockpiled and a contingent of armed guards had been stationed to guard the stone building holding the animal feed as well as basic staples for their own human consumption. For months, the wives had been sun-drying foods for storage in clay jars.

Shem stated the obvious, "We have most things ready. But, there are two major challenges left. First, who is going to join us in the ark? And, how do we gather the animals?"

"We have been pleading with the city for, well, as long as I can remember." Ham said. "Maybe we should have one last special event at the gate and let that be it. If they come, they come."

Noah sat looking at the others, slowly nodding his head, wanting to agree. There was a limit to the old preacher's patience. What more could he do? What more could he say? He had a hard time replying. Emotions he didn't know he had welled up and he began to cry. He stood and spread out his arms as though he were catching something falling from above.

"Have I not been bold enough? Should I have been more clear? How have I failed these people?" he said with tears. "I can't believe the Lord God wants even *one* of these souls to perish! They are wicked. Yes! And completely hostile to the ways of God. Yes! But as God is infinitely just and good, he is also infinitely merciful!"

He calmed a bit and lowered his arms. "But, it seems we've been called to preach. So. . . ."

The old, tired man sat and rested his hands on the table.

Shem spoke up. "Let's have one last time at the gate, like Ham says. You can preach or I can."

Then he looked at Ham. "Or, Maybe Ham, *you* can preach?"

126

Ham looked terrified.

They all laughed. It felt good to laugh at such a moment. Everything hung in some great cosmic balance, but peace settled on them knowing they had, indeed, done all they could. They had built the ark and had not been secretive about what it was for. The people knew. Everyone knew. But, they would give it one last try the next day at the gate. Possibly the finality of it would persuade the people to act.

"So, then, what about the animals?" Ham asked.

"There is no way we can go get them," Noah said. "I believe they must come to us."

"But how do they know when and where to show up?" Japheth asked.

By this time unanswerable questions and impossible problems like this had become routine.

Noah stood with that look on his face he always had when he was going to pray. They all stood.

"Lord God," he prayed softly, "you said the animals *must* come. So, they *will* come. Male and female they will come. You have spoken. We put our trust in you for all that lies ahead. The ground is shaking, Lord. Even as I pray, I can feel the earth groan. We can also feel your presence with us. Help us accomplish your will. And Lord, open the ears of the people tomorrow. If they reject you, Lord, we are confident that what you do will be just and right. Amen."

And they all said, "Amen."

28

The People's Last Chance

Word spread in the city that Noah had something to say. Not many were inclined to cross the bridge and listen to him. They had grown tired of Noah.

For over a hundred years they had put up with his fantasy, his useless ark, his preoccupation with traditions from old worn-out myths of the distant past. Life in the land had become unbearable and it took every ounce of energy to protect and hold on to what little was left. The drought, the dust, the shaking, the violence, the chaos! In a land where no one had ever felt completely secure, violence between groups had intensified. There was not a shred of goodwill among men. Information had become so controlled by those in power, no one could grasp what was true. The economy was in shambles. The only industry in the city that was truly thriving was the iron works, where they forged blades, locks and iron bars.

So, that morning, only a few showed up at Noah's gate. There were no officials or chief merchants among them. It was mostly the poor and unemployed who had little else to do. And one Alya, who pushed his way to the front. He was thin and looked weak. His long hair hung to the back of his knees, but it was not caked with dung as usual. He did not have the usual, dark and cunning countenance of the Alya. Rather, he stood there looking up at Noah as a broken man, lost and helpless.

Noah and Shem stood together at the front edge of the platform in the "safe space" by the side of the gate entrance. They had met and counseled many at that place. This meeting would likely be their last. Some of the small crowd gathered before them had heard Noah preach many times and had come again as hecklers and scoffers. A few had met there privately with Noah or Shem, when they needed someone to arbitrate some grievance. Some came priding themselves as seekers, open to new religious ideas that they could integrate into their belief system.

This day, only the Alya man stood there out of genuine need. He had never known peace living in the world of spirits and had sensed in Noah a higher authority. Perhaps he could be set free from the voices in his head, somehow.

"Thank you all for coming," Noah began. "I have been preaching from this place for over a hundred years. None of you need to hear me again. You know I am going to tell you again of the God of Creation who knows you and desires to be known. Again, I remind you to look around and see that the magnificence of the created world is undeniably the work of an Almighty God. I can say again that he is personal, that he walked and talked with Adam and Eve and desires to walk with you and me. But are your ears open to what I have to say? I can remind you of his goodness, mercy and justice, qualities that never change and qualities of character he wants to instill in each of us. Shem could step forward and tell you again that each of us must take ourself off the throne of our life and allow God to be Lord of all. God of Creation desires our friendship. But our words, like seeds, have fallen on barren ground. The soil of your hearts has grown harder. And I am afraid God has decided he cannot reap a harvest among you. His patience is at an end.

"But listen to me! Floodwaters are coming. This day is your last chance to turn all that you are, or ever hope to be, over to the living God."

Then, Noah said something that would remain in Shem's thoughts as a marvelous mystery.

"Look upon it my friends." Noah said, turning toward the ark which could be seen looming above the wall in the distance. "Look, see it with different eyes. Believe and be saved! God has made the most vital thing easy. Do not choose the hard way of self and miss life."

There was a long pause and a man from the back yelled, "Is that it then Noah? Is that all you've got? If you ask me, you should lock yourself in that ark so we can be done with you!"

Nearly everyone laughed.

There was a group of three men standing together in the crowd. They had been regulars at Noah's gatherings. One raised his hand and yelled, "So, this god of yours needs our friendship, does he? Sounds rather needy to me!" His friends chimed in, "Yeah!"

Shem answered, "He doesn't need any of us. He is all sufficient within himself. But he desires our friendship and obedience."

"Obedience, huh?" the man shot back. "Sounds to me more like a tyrant than a friendly sort of god."

"You would find him to be no tyrant, my friend," Shem replied. "You would find that he gives much more than he requires of those he loves."

"Well, all I need is more requirements," the man said. "I have a wife! I don't need anyone else telling me what I can't do."

His friends thought that was awfully funny and had a good laugh.

He went on, "Well, you folks up there on the platform think you're pretty righteous. Well, I'm a good person, if that's what you're getting at. I don't beat my wife no more and ain't killed anybody. At least not for a while."

That got another big laugh and a hard slap on the back from his friends.

"May I ask you a question?" Shem asked.

"I suppose if it ain't too hard."

"If someone wanted to befriend you, but you wanted no part of it and swore never to return the friendship because it would require too much of you, would you expect that person's love and loyalty?"

"No. Suppose not."

"And," Shem went on, "if you, because of your own sins, found yourself over your head in trouble, would you expect that person to save you, even if he could?"

"I don't need no saving from anybody. Certainly not from that tyrant god of yours if that's what you're gettin' at!"

Shem replied, quite forcefully, "When that time comes, my friend, you will remember those words with bitter sorrow!"

Shem's exchange with the man seemed to give the crowd pause. There were a few more, somewhat less sarcastic remarks and some pushing and shoving and the crowd began to break up.

The Alya man held his place in the ebbing flow of the crowd, then stepped forward, put his hand on the edge of the platform and looked up at Shem. He stood there saying nothing. Shem crouching at the edge of the platform said, "I know who you are. I talked to you when I was a young man. Do you remember me?"

"No. But, I see in you something all other men lack. Though others mock you, I desire to have what you have."

Noah descended the steps and came over to the man, laid his hand on his shoulder and asked him if he could pray for him. The man nodded and hung his head. Noah prayed a short prayer about God's power, about sin, deliverance and freedom and made specific demands and rather harsh commands, which, when said, shook the man, causing him to convulse and cry out. Then he crumpled to the ground and lay there weeping.

Shem descended from the platform, kneeled by the man and said, "Come with us. You must or you will be lost."

The man stood before the other two, placed his palms together and bowed. "I am indebted to you. Thank you. I owe you my life. You have repaid my treachery with kindness. The true God of Creation is with you."

"Then, come with us," Shem said. "Live for God now in righteousness. You no longer need to obey the spirits of this world, but can now serve and obey the Living God."

"Yes," the man said. "But, first I must put my affairs in order. I have a brother who depends on me, who would worry about me. I am so sorry."

He then backed slowly away, apologizing and said, for sure, he would come back.

So, all were gone. Noah and Shem walked back to their homes and continued packing their things.

The ark was finished. They had done all they could do.

29

The Animals Come

Around the world, every living creature stopped.
A mother bear in her den, a goat on a rocky ledge, a sparrow tending to her nest, a mole burrowing in the sod, a hippopotamus wallowing in the mud, a velociraptor hiding in a cave, a primate peeling a banana, a large cat stalking a wild ox, all stopped, lifted their heads and held their breath. They could feel it more than hear it. Something had changed or was about to change. It was not a vibration or a sound. They had felt the tremors. But this was not that. It was a knowing. Each of them and millions of others, turned their attention away from their normal patterns and began to prepare. Something was coming and they knew it.

Mice began to hoard seeds. Ducks nestled together in the bullrushes. Deer moved to the swamp and lay hidden in the tall grass. Moles stopped burrowing new tunnels and huddled with their mates.

While most were hunkering down, individual pairs of every kind began to wander off and away from the others. They left their families and usual feeding grounds and, guided by a delicately calibrated inner compass, followed unmarked paths to unknown places over unfamiliar horizons. Male and female moved together, foraging along the way, in no hurry, some accompanied by their young, unable to resist the strange, inner calling to go. Their natural instincts had been, for some reason, altered and they were carried off by an unfamiliar impulse. It was not an escape from fear. It was a journey to hope.

In pairs they moved, coming from all directions converging on the river and forested regions of the land of Noah. As birds and butterflies navigate the invisible paths of the air, they came. Walking, hopping, flying. Some from the far side of the distant sea. Some from the tropics. Some from the desert plains. Large and small. Some so large they shook the earth. Others were hardly large enough to be noticed. All of every kind that had breath were moving. They were led by an unseen hand.

Early one morning, as Noah opened the back gate of the compound and began down his trail and as Shem went out to check on the cattle pens, they both noticed two deer drinking at the edge of the river, and shockingly, a pair of canines standing nearby, and groups of other animals lingering about in the field. Several large, unknown kinds of birds perched on the compound wall, and the trees were filled with a noisy flock of birds of a variety Shem had not seen before.

Shem called out to his father in a loud voice, causing the cattle to bolt to the far side of the stall, "Father! Your prayer was answered! Look around!"

Noah looked up, waved and shouted something Shem could not hear.

When Noah got down to his bench, he found it occupied by two large, very strange lizards warming themselves in the early morning sun. They were coming.

30

Entering the Ark

It was late in the afternoon the day after the animals were first seen. Japheth's wife, Anahit, was sitting at her table with stacks of clay tablets laid out before her. She moved the oil lamp closer so she could better see the markings on each of the clay tablets. Each had rows of markings, each row representing a different kind, or family of animals.

She had, since early childhood, had a keen interest in animal life and had spent many enjoyable hours with Methuselah, Lamech and other elders who had traveled far and had recollection of animals from regions beyond her own. Minds were sharp in those days and many had broad, detailed understanding of the animal world. Tradition was clear that God named the stars, but had left Adam with the monumental task of naming the animals. That meant he had to acquire a detailed understanding of the physical distinctions between living creatures. He named them according to families and specific kinds of animals and was careful to pass this knowledge on to each generation. Adam had a long life, over nine-hundred years, and had much time to explore and learn.

The tablets were organized in stacks on the table. Each stack represented a different area on one of the three decks in the ark. There were assigned stalls for mammals, large, medium and small. Nets were suspended to create spaces for birds of different types. There were the special cages for reptiles and the creatures that lived in water as well as on land. And there were sturdy cages for aggressive critters, such as giant reptiles, which she knew could only come as juveniles, so she hoped adults would come with their small newborns or, possibly, with eggs. There would be pairs of bears, cats, rodents, wolves and so on. These would eventually interbreed and produce many varieties. Using the knowledge she had, she restricted the passengers to "kinds," as God had directed. And, she advised Japheth on the number, location and size of stalls needed in the ark.

Now that animals were coming in, they would know if her calculations were correct. She was eager to help with getting them onboard in some kind of orderly fashion. She and Ham had driven a large number of poles into the ground leading up to the ramp and had connected the poles by hemp rope creating holding stalls and guide paths. This, she hoped, would help organize the loading of animals, keep them from wandering around the compound and provide holding areas for different types waiting to be taken in and brought to their stalls. She had placed buckets of water, grain, green plants and fruits which she guessed could be used to lure the animals in and keep them content.

Anahit had only a vague idea just how many animals would come, but she had done her best to prepare. God had specified the size of the ark and, therefore, she could assume there would be ample room. She had calculated that there would be more than a thousand different kinds. Of course, there would be no fish, whales or aquatic animals that could survive in water. She figured the ark could hold several thousand passengers, plus a few extra "clean animals" which God had directed Noah to take. This was likely for food for the humans and for what God may have planned after the flood.

Japheth came into the room out of breath, "They're really coming in now! We can start loading the first critters tonight if you think that'll work."

"Why not?" she answered. "We can't let them pile up by the river. Start loading the animals that move by day . The nocturnal animals will be here later. Load the birds last. Keep the predators separate. You'll have to separate the adult, giant reptiles from their young. Good luck with that!"

Japheth, Shem and Ham worked into the night with servants to direct the animals as they wandered in from the fields or crossed the river. For the most part, the pairs that came stayed together and could be directed along the roped-off paths, up the ramp and into the ark. There was a steady stream of animals moving up and in. Inside, Noah's cattlemen and shepherds, pushed and prodded the squealing, squawking critters up and down passageways and into stalls.

Noah stood by the door with his walking stick encouraging passengers that hesitated at the threshold.

It was a sight to behold! Noah was smiling and repeatedly calling out to Japheth that he could not believe what was happening.

"This is just too much to believe, Japheth! I mean, God said they would come. But to see these animals actually coming is too much!"

Animals that he had never seen were standing before him pawing the ground waiting to enter. Animals with long necks, animals that waddled along, animals with flat tails, long tails or no tails. Animals with short fur, spikey fur, or no fur. Animals with large curly horns, big droopy ears, long pointy teeth. One can only imagine Noah's emotions at this moment. The menagerie of animals before him was enough to create a sense of awe. And the fact that what God had said was coming to pass, before his eyes, in the nick of time, was more wonder than he could contain.

Much later that same night, when Noah and his wife sat down, exhausted, on the edge of their bed, Noah said with a sigh, "I have seen much in my lifetime. I've heard much from my father and grandfather about wonderful things God has done in the past. God has spoken to me directly and told me amazing things. But I've never seen or experienced anything like what we saw tonight."

"We'd better get some sleep," Nayiri said.

"I know. But, just think! The whole kingdom of animals responding to a supernatural call of God! All right before our eyes. Some must have been traveling for weeks. There they were, walking up the ramp. To be honest, my dear," he said putting his arm around her shoulders, "until tonight, I wasn't sure, I wasn't *completely* sure they'd come. But now, I've seen the power of God with my own eyes. And now, the waters will come. And soon!"

139

Did you know? *God commanded Noah to bring into the ark "two of every kind" of bird, animal and creature. "Kind" differs from the modern term "species" and may be approximated by the modern designation "genus" or "family." So, a pair of canines, representing one Kind or Family, kept alive in the ark and then released, would eventually generate, over time, multiple species such as wolf, dog, coyote, etc., all of which can interbreed. Therefore, the size of the ark was sufficient to hold two of every known family of animals, even dinosaurs, especially if the very small, young ones were selected.*

31

Closing the Door

Just days later, God said to Noah, "Go into the ark, you and your whole family, because I have found you righteous in this generation. In seven days, the flood will come."

Noah spread the word in the compound and gathered everyone together.

He said, "Today we enter the ark, seal the door and wait. The animals and all provisions are in. A flood is coming in seven days. It will rain for forty days and nights. This the Lord God has said. He told us to build an ark, and we did. He said the animals would come, and they came. He said the waters will come, and they will come. So, I'm inviting everyone here, family, servants, laborers and all to come. Enter the ark with us and spare your lives."

He, his sons and their wives stepped forward and formed a small group at the base of the ramp. The others mumbled amongst themselves for several minutes, then dispersed toward the gate and their homes. A few of the older servants, who had been with Noah a long time, lingered near the ark unable to decide. But, their younger family members pulled the older ones away toward the main gate. A sentry was sent by Noah to the gate to see if there was anyone there who may have had a change of heart. He especially wanted to see if the Alya man had decided to come.

After some minutes the sentry returned and informed Noah no one was at the gate, but that he saw the Alya man standing a ways off in his distinctive orange cloth, just this side of the bridge.

"I called to him, sir," the sentry said. "I told him you were entering the ark. I think he heard me. But he just waved as if to say there was something in the city he needed to attend to, sir."

"Ok, then, thank you."

The sentry, a long-time servant of Noah, bowed before Noah, knelt and kissed his master's feet, a custom of deep respect. Then, with a sad look, turned and walked toward the gate with his turban in his hands.

During this whole scene there were background noises one might expect from thousands of animals of all kinds caged in a strange, new, wooden world. Cattle were stomping, horses neighing, elephants trumpeting, cats screaming, primates chattering, birds calling.

To anyone outside the ark, if there had been anyone, those sounds would have suddenly stopped, when the family entered the ark and the door was shut. They would have heard Ham drive four tapered wooden wedges into their slots, drawing the door up tight against its seals.

There were no grand gestures or speeches. Everything had been done and everything there was to say had been said. It was time now for the earth to release its waters and for the righteous few to see the saving grace of God.

32

The Earth Convulses

The dust and super-heated gases spewing into the high atmosphere, dimming the sun and darkening the sky over Noah's land, were just the early indications of something far greater about to happen. The quiet earth was awakening from its centuries-long slumber since creation. In the deepest part of a distant ocean a seam in the earth's crust was beginning to shift. No created being knows where the energy came to begin the move, but a large tectonic plate of the earth began to move against its neighboring plate. Rather than slide laterally a few inches, as it had been doing for a number of years causing tremors, it began to dive downward and under. In a matter of minutes, it encountered the molten rock below, lifted up the edge of an entire continent, opened up a thousand-mile gap in the crust and released a massive flow of white-hot magma into the cold waters of the sea.

On the far side of Noah's planet, a thousand cubic miles of ocean water exploded into the ice-cold atmosphere where it turned instantly into a storm of water and ice. Clouds, larger and higher and filled with more moisture than had ever been seen on the earth, were carried along by high winds over the sea toward land.

The downward moving plate continued downward where its melted mass began to disrupt portions of the outer, molten core. Currents in the water-thin molten core boiled upward against the fractured   crust like a great pot of porridge. Volcanos erupted along the length of these fissures forming new lands and islands on the earth where just hours or days before, there had been open sea or open plains. Edges of the earth's plates began to press against each other and mountain ranges were raised up as plates moving at high speed crashed into each other.

The sea, now boiling with its intensely hot and freezing cold regions, became the mother of a hundred hurricanes bearing more rain than the world had ever seen or would ever see again. Until some kind of equilibrium was reached in the dynamic upheaval of the earth's crust and atmosphere, the sea would remain a tempest and the rain would continue.

And the storms continued to move overland toward the land of Noah.

33

Inside the Ark

Ham, and Japheth's wife, Anahit, went together up and down the length of the ark inspecting the animal cages making sure all the passengers were in their places and getting along with their neighbors.

"I can't believe this is happening!" Ham told her as they moved along the passageway. "I've had my doubts, I'll admit. But when the animals came the other day, that was, well, how do you explain something like that?"

They stopped by the cage of a pair of small spotted deer. The two animals pressed their noses through slots in the gate and snorted. Anahit picked up a hand-full of dried grass and held it to their outstretched tongues. Ham reached over the gate and scratched the female's head and patted her on the neck. She looked back at him with large watery eyes and leaned into his touch.

"I don't know if they're all going to be this friendly," she said.

They descended to the bottom deck and stood before the two largest animals they had ever seen.

"And to think these are only babies!" Anahit said. "They are elephants."

One of the animals reached a long, wrinkled trunk over the gate and took hold of Ham's turban, took it off him and pitched it down the passageway where it slid under the gate of another cage. Ham ran and reached under the gate to retrieve it.

"Ouch!" he yelled as he pulled out the turban with a badly scratched hand.

"Oh, that's the big cat," Anahit told him laughing. "We'll have to be sure they don't get loose. If they get out we could be short a few animals when we get to where we're going."

They double-checked the cat's cage, tightened the netting around the top and continued checking on the others.

Noah and the family went to ready their living quarters where they had moved their basic furniture, beds and personal necessities. It was a small, rectangular room on the top deck near the front of the vessel where there was light and fresh air from the gap under the roof. The women had put down carpets and hung up woven partitions offering privacy for the four couples. The walls of their space were the only solid wooden walls in the ark. No one wanted animals or birds poking their heads in or getting at their food. Japheth had hung bronze oil lamps from beams and fastened iron hand-holds at several points along the walls.

"It could get pretty rough," he had said. "We'll need something to hang on to."

It was Shem's idea to suspend hammocks instead of using their usual for-legged beds to conserve on space and to be better in a moving environment. None of them had slept in such a thing, but it made practical sense.

"When father and I were out at the coast, we saw sailors using hammocks," Shem told them. "Seems like it would work for us."

Thoughts of being in a moving vessel, having to hold on to hand-holds and sleeping in a swinging hammock were not appealing thoughts. There was a lot of nervous laughter and joking around. The strange environment with the animal sounds, the stomping of hoofs, the screeching of primates, birds and thousands of home-sick critters was unnerving. And the smells. For the time being, the fresh smell of the aromatic cedar wood that Japheth had lined the living quarters with was enough to subdue some of the strong animal smells, but that would probably change.

That first night in the ark, to everyone's surprise, was rather enjoyable. They lit the lamps, sat around on the carpets, ate flat bread with olive oil and herbs that Nayiri had prepared and talked about all the events of the past years. They could almost forget, for the moment, the terror that approached. Increasingly severe tremors shook the timbers. But they put their minds on the work at hand. They discussed a schedule for feeding the animals and disposing of waste. Before they slept, each couple took their turn making rounds through the ark to check on the animals to be sure each one was getting its water supplied by one of three very large water tanks on the top deck, which, they were hoping, would not run out before the rains came.

Outside the ark, fierce cold winds were driving thick, dark clouds over the face of an orange moon. Leaves and small branches were flying through the air against the buildings of the compound. A loose gate on a cattle pen was slamming against its post, over and over. Most people of the city were staying in their shuttered homes around the hearth for warmth and security. Women held their little ones. Men cursed at themselves, at others and at their gods for having allowed such troubled times. That Noah! Ever since he started building that wicked thing! He's probably sitting in that ark right now laughing. He thinks his god is going to destroy us all, huh? Well, he's not going to get rid of us that easy!

The desperate went to the temple. The priests were busy into the night burning offerings on old, broken charred altars and reciting ancient prayers surrounded by frightened worshippers that came from their homes, even on such a cold, blustery night. The ground was shaking, the sky was lit by flashing lights and fear gripped their hearts. Life had become a confusing, frustrating and surreal thing! The sky! The shaking! The drought! That Noah and the dark, ominous object jutting up over his wall! The priest better have a solution! He'd better get some god to help us or we'll offer him up on that altar!

As they sheltered, the hurricanes were moving. They had spent most of their violent energy traveling over vast plains of the continent. But they carried great quantities of moisture inland along with dust and gases collected along the way from long ridges of newly forming volcanoes.

34

Shut In

The animals had quit their initial wailing and complaining about their restricted quarters. When they knew they were secure, they mostly sat staring at their gates waiting for their morning and afternoon feeding. Or, they just slept. To the family's surprise, an unexpected peace settled over the ark after the first few days. They got into a routine of feeding, watering and cleaning stalls. Small animals that squeezed through gaps were roaming freely. It was impossible to keep everything and everyone in their place.

God had told Noah that the rain would come in seven days. Since the animals had come as he said, the family expected the rains to come on time. But, late in the evening of the sixth day, only dry, dusty winds buffeted the hull of the ark as they had on the first day. Little had changed. Would the waters come?

They sat in their quarters under the oil lamps talking about what might happen next.

"We made sure all the scaffolding and supports were detached," Ham said. "So, my guess is the thing will lift off pretty smooth. Water will fill the pit, but it won't float quite yet. Water will have to get up to about the second deck level before she'll lift off."

Noah asked, "Will the door seals keep the water out?"

"The door is high on the side," Japheth said. "But no doubt it will get plenty of water. We laid in two beads of pitch-soaked twisted wool. Ham said it was pulled up tight and wedged. So it'll hold."

Shem asked, "What do we do if someone wants to get in?"

No one had a ready answer for that. It would be a dangerous thing to open the door when the waters were rising. Folks had had their chance. But it would be a sad affair.

Then Ham spoke. "I don't think we could open the door if we wanted to."

"Why is that?" Noah asked.

"When we swung the door closed on its hinges, it drew *itself* up tight against its seals, before I drove the wedges. I can't explain it, but I don't think the door can be opened from the inside."

"That settles the matter." Noah said. "The Lord has shut us in. As for the others, I think it is more about belief than survival. You and I have put faith in God's words to us, faith in who he is and has always been. If someone comes, pounds on the door because they've chosen to put their faith in God, we would hoist them over the side if necessary. But, if they see the waters rise and come to save their own skin, then they must live with their choice."

"Sadly," Anahit added, "they will die with their choice."

"Makes me think of Adam's choice," Ham said looking at the others.

"Vipers will flee from a fire." Noah said. "But that doesn't mean you take them into your heart. Their bite is still deadly."

It was the end of a very long day. With the sounds of wind and the soft stirring of animals, they drew the woven partitions and settled into their hammocks. Many decades of planning, preaching, preparing, building and wondering had led up to this moment. They lay there unable to sleep. How will the rains come? They had never seen hard rain. Where will we end up? How long will the journey last? What will life be like after all this? What must it be like for the people of the city?

As they were laying there pondering these thoughts, Noah slipped out of his hammock, quietly opened the door from the living quarters and followed the dark passageway toward the front of the ark. He had discovered a small, private space there between cages where he could sit on a beam and see up through the netting to get a glimpse of the sky. This had become his place of prayer. He sat there for some minutes watching the dark clouds roll by.

"We built it," he said to God. "We finished the ark you told us to build. And now, we are completely dependent upon you. Watch over us. Where can we find safety but in you? You are our only refuge at a time such as this. The world has put their trust in themselves and are lost. But we trust in you. Thank you for your mercy and unchanging goodness. Keep us Lord! Keep my family and all these creatures in the safety of your mighty hands!"

He sat there trying to maintain a sense of peace about what was to come. For several minutes he recalled what he knew of the Creator's words and actions of the past. He thought about Adam and Eve and how the Creator had walked in the garden in the cool of the day and asked them, "Where are you?" Adam answered, "I heard you in the garden, and I was afraid because I was naked." Adam had eaten of the forbidden tree and was condemned by his own guilt and afraid.

Both Methuselah and his father had talked of this to Noah. Why are we so uncomfortable in God's presence? Why do we hide? Is it because he is a threat? No, it is because of our own unrighteousness before him. Our guilt separates us.

Noah looked up at the stormy sky. "My God, because of your great grace and through your help I have lived a righteous life before you. I have walked in your ways. Though I have failed many times, I have looked for you, listened for you, searched for you. And you have always met me with a sense of your presence. No, it isn't me who has gone looking for you, but it is *you* who has sought *me* out and chose to bless me with your presence all these years.

"Now, you bring righteous judgement onto the earth and all its people. I don't know if we will survive your anger. Nevertheless, your will be done. We commit ourselves into your hands."

Noah slipped back into the quarters.

As he settled awkwardly into his hammock, a heavy mass of cold air from the northeast began its descent into the land of Noah and the lands to the west. There it met the warm, moist hurricane air being driven inland from the heated and churning sea. Thunderheads rose and began unloading their moisture onto the land as they swept across the continent.

At the same time, the part of the earth's crust that had descended into the core, had begun to force molten rock upward against the adjacent plate beneath the sea. As the plate lifted, the level of the sea all along its edge rose instantly releasing its energy into a giant wave, miles high. The wave moved across the surface reaching land in hours where it swept away the distant port city Noah and Shem had visited. In seconds the wave devastated everything along the coast. It continued to flow inland toward the hill country west of Noah's land carrying everything with it in a mile-thick mat of sea water, rock, mud and vegetation. The wave would not reach Noah's compound, but it pushed the river system eastward flooding his western lands.

Molten rock from the hot core continued to pour into waters of the sea. Since hot rock displaces more space than cold earth, waters of the sea were pushed up and over the edges of the earth's lands.

Peals of thunder shook the ark and woke the passengers. Not a living creature had ever heard such a sound. Lightening flashed in streaks through the interior of the ark. The buffeting wind now struck the wooden hull and roof with such force to cause the entire vessel to shudder. In a land watered by quiet mists, these sounds were strange and terrifying.

Ham and Japheth both ran to the nearest access to the window at the very top of the ark and looked out at the scene. Trees were bent in the wind. Pieces of the outer wall tumbled through the compound and cattle still in the pen were sheltering behind the shed. It was nearly impossible to see the city through the dust that whipped through the compound and across the river.

Shem joined them. "What do we do?" he asked.

"Nothing we can do," Ham said. "We wait."

"I suggest we stay with father and the women," Japheth added. "Try to keep our minds occupied. Try to sleep if we can. Tomorrow is going to be. . .well, unusual."

They tried to offer a smile, then made a quick inspection of the vessel and returned to their quarters.

They lay in their hammocks, wide awake, listening to the beating sound of heavy winds, hoofs pawing on wood and the pulse of their own beating hearts.

That same night, the great system of springs that had been quietly welling up for centuries to feed the river system of the continent, erupted into something many times its original size. From several fountains a tremendously increased volume of water flowed upward, out of hidden places in the earth, to the surface. Very soon, the river that passed between Noah's compound and the city would not only be swollen by these erupting springs, but also by the waters pushed onto land from the west.

Meanwhile, the jarring and colliding of plates of the earth's crust, far from human sight and beyond knowing, was setting fiery hot against icy cold, unstoppable masses of rock against immovable continents of stone. What was at the bottom of the sea would soon be found on tops of the earth's highest mountains as the original, created layers of the earth were bent and heaved into a landscape impossible to comprehend.

Water from above and below, enough to cover the earth, was coming. Storms were drawing up moisture from the sea and depositing it on land. Fountains of the deep were bringing to the surface water never before seen. And, most importantly, movement of the earth's plates was causing pressure to force the bed of the ocean upward, while the land broke into multiple continents and was pushed downward making it feasible for water to cover the entire planet. The proportion of land to sea was changing, as well as the shape and number of land masses. This would take some time, but not eons, just weeks and months.

But that sixth night in the ark, the family of eight saw only four wooden walls and some swinging oil lamps. They were no more aware of the geological forces at play across the earth than the modern professor, many centuries later, who finds sea shells in mysteriously sloping sedimentary rock high in the mountains. Noah would get a good chuckle out of the professor's explanations scrawled out in chalk on a blackboard. Neither would know the particulars, but Noah knew the probable cause. He knew the words of the Lord of Creation and the time over which it occurred. From those facts, he could draw intelligent conclusions and develop meaningful theories.

As for the eight laying in their hammocks, they were hoping for a nice hard rain and a gentle lift-off, not a journey into some kind of rolling, pitching wildlife adventure.

35

The Rain

On the morning of the seventh day the rains hit.

Noah had slipped out of the living quarters and gone to his place on the beam. The sustained, deep murmuring of the wind against the ark had put the others to sleep. But Noah couldn't sleep. He had God's words repeating in his head, "Seven days from now I will send rain on the earth for forty days and forty nights." He could visualize what rain was, but had never experienced more than the kind of rain he saw that fell on the slopes of the high hills after harvest.

At first it sounded like someone was tapping to get his attention. Then it sounded like a bowl of dried beans had spilled and were falling from a table to the wooden floor. Then, in a matter of seconds, it was like the whole bag of beans was being poured out in a roar of sound. Water began to strike Noah in the face as rain drops hit the framework of the window above and fell on him.

He yelled, "Japheth! It's the seventh day!"

His excitement was less about the extraordinary weather event happening outside, than about the amazing timing and reliability of the word of his God. The animals had come! The rain is here! Now the flood will come! He was not unaware of the irony of it.

"Why am I thrilled to see the hand of the Lord moving," he asked himself, "though it be to sweep me away and destroy all I know?"

Nayiri came up beside him.

"Noah, we may want to remember this day. This is the seventeenth day of the sixth month of your six-hundredth year."

Noah just shook his head. That is something a woman would remember, he thought.

Japheth and the others all came rushing down the passageway and spread out along the rail where they could see out through the long window that ran the length of both sides of the ark just under the roof. They pushed aside the netting that kept flying critters from getting out, held out their hands and played like children in the rain. They could look down and see that the cartwheel tracks in the compound were already filling with water and puddles were forming everywhere.

Then Ham yelled and pointed beyond the back of the ark, "Hey, look what's coming!"

Just beyond the building field, a mass of black mud and debris had filled the entire river channel, and was flowing slowly around the curve of the compound toward the bridge. As it moved it expanded methodically over the banks, quickly sweeping away the woven willow outer wall and the buildings on that side of the compound.

Earlier that day, the erupting spring had flooded the hill country dislodging soil, rock and vegetation, and carried it all downward through Noah's fields and into the local rivers and streams. Mud snaked in an eerie mass around the compound and began to pile up against the bridge.

Ham yelled again. "Look who's at the bridge!"

Through the driving rain, they all could see a person, hesitating on the east side of the river near the bridge, obviously very frightened of the growing mass of tree limbs and mud that was beginning to heave up and over and onto the bridge. The man tried once, then twice to make it across toward the ark, but retreated just as the bridge gave way and the entire, black mud flow rapidly began to spread over the space between the city and the compound. The man retreated, falling and stumbling backward, uphill toward the city to escape. At the city gate he turned and looked. Noah's family could just see a faint glimpse of him through the rain. He was bare-chested and wore a simple orange loin cloth.

While the others were watching the spectacle out the window, both Shem and Noah had slipped away and were conversing down by Noah's beam. No one knows what they were talking about, but their heads were bowed, they were talking softly and Noah kept shaking his head. Shem seemed to be consoling him.

Noah's river now swelled further with rain water from the surrounding watershed. By the evening of the seventh day, as Japheth and the others watched the flood grow, they could no longer see much of the compound, its walls and buildings. Everything had been swept away in the current that flowed in the direction of the river on its way to the delta. There were just a few stout oak trees, some remaining posts from the scaffolding used to build the ark and the very top of the stone safe-house wall. Their homes, the cattle, the stacks of left-over beams and planks, the gate and bridge were all below the surface of churning, muddy water. And strange as it may seem, even during the rain and flood, the earth moved and trembled enough to shake the ark and send waves across the water.

That night was a night of little sleep. In addition to the constant drone of pouring rain on the roof, there were loud thumps and crashes as heavy, floating objects struck the hull and scraped along the side. And there were the tremors that continued. Even the animals stirred and seemed uneasy, pawing the floor and moaning.

In the early light of the next day, one at a time, each member of the family went to the window to see. Nothing at all remained of the compound, not even the very top of the tallest pines. The river was gone. A body of slow-moving water stretched from the ark in the compound eastward up the hill to the city wall a half mile away. Water had reached the gate at the south end of the city which was the highest point in the area. Further north, as the family looked to their left, the water had risen over the city wall and had obviously flooded most of the town. The road leading out of the main gate was filled with townspeople moving in a long line toward the land to the south. But there was no higher ground in that direction, just a small knoll, which looked to be already crowded with persons fleeing the flood. And the water was steadily rising.

All that day and into the evening the family visited the window between chores. By sundown, nothing of the city could be seen except the stone tower at the top of the ruler's palace. The very top branches of the pine trees by Noah's walk were now under the surface. Aside from the ark and ruler's tower, nothing of the world remained in sight. And the rain continued in a steady downpour.

It happened in the early morning hours of the next day.

Nayiri had unwrapped a loaf of flatbread and was breaking it up and laying pieces around a cloth she had laid out on the floor. The family was reclined in a circle to say morning prayers and eat the morning meal, when the ark lurched abruptly to the side. Noah fell over into Shem's lap. There were several loud crashes as animals caught off balance fell to the deck. Anahit quickly gathered up the corners of the cloth and collected the bread as everyone tried to stand and make their way to the window.

They were afloat and slowly drifting southward with the current. At least, they thought it must be southward, but then, there were no landmarks visible in the rain to judge direction. They could not see the western hills. The tower was gone. The flood had come full force and swept them away.

Japheth hollered to the brothers, "Go around. Check everything! Take some wool and a chinking tool and stop any leaks!"

They were pleased to see that the ark, with all the weight it carried, was riding nicely on the water with the amount of free-board they expected. But if the water got rough, what then?

They were soon to find out.

Disturbances in the earth's crust continued to alter the shape of continents, force sea water unto land and lift moisture into the atmosphere. The colliding of tectonic plates caused the redistribution of sea water and the creation of dramatic ocean currents flowing in new and unusual patterns. All the while, the moon was pulling waters west to east as it passed through the night sky. There was little chance the ark, drifting uncontrolled in rapidly moving waters, could avoid danger, for they were utterly unprepared and knew nothing of what lay ahead.

At the moment, the flood around them carried the ark in a steady, upright manner. But, beyond the horizon, they could face rip currents, tsunami waves and thick masses of floating vegetation drifting in thousand-mile long rafts upon the sea. There was a vast number of dangers known only to the God of Noah who had touched the earth and brought the flood.

And the rain kept coming.

Did you know? *It is not possible for the earth's atmosphere to hold enough moisture in the form of rain to cover the earth with enough water to cover the mountains. However, if the earth's crust shifted, pushing the water of the ocean basins up and onto land, then it is feasible. Also, it is well known, that hidden in the earth's crust is a vast store of groundwater. Ninety-five percent of all fresh water is underground.*

36

Afloat

Drifting along on the current the ark moved through pouring rain upon a surface cluttered with everything from land that would float. During those first few days of riding the flood, the family stayed mostly in their quarters or stayed intentionally busy caring for the passengers. It was not pleasant to think much about the reality of the situation, to be packed into an untested wooden vessel adrift on an endless sea of unknown dangers. Only Noah dared look out the window. Perhaps it was because the fresh air and a look at the horizon calmed his stomach.

Disturbances in the earth's surface far below the waters caused large masses of energy to sweep across the surface of the flood. But, fortunately, the tsunami waves did not come as abrupt breakers which could turn over or damage the ark.

Rather, they came as tremendously large, rolling swells of the sea that lifted the ark abruptly, throwing everyone off balance and then in the descent, causing everyone's stomach to rise in their throats, a new and frightening experience for all. The animals would make a racket as each wave hit. The elephants had gotten into the habit of trumpeting when the ark rocked and the big cats let out a loud, low scream. A person could feel the wind of the birds' wings as they all left their perches at the same time and settled back again.

For forty days the rain poured as the ark rocked steadily on the waters of the flood.

Then, one morning, the family woke to the quiet murmuring of the animals. The rain had stopped and the surface of the flood had calmed. The view from the window seemed almost strange as they looked out at a brilliantly pink sky to the east reflecting off the surface of a muddy sea. The scattered clutter of debris had gathered itself into large floating islands strung out along the edges of ocean currents. The sky above was a dusty gray. The rising sun could not be clearly seen on the muddled horizon, but it was good to see that the dark rain clouds had dispersed. The air near the surface had been washed clean, but high in the atmosphere, there was the dust and smoke from volcanoes still active somewhere on the other side of the earth. The tectonic plates of the earth had paused in their grinding and colliding. Some kind of equilibrium had been reached in the balance of energy across the surface of the planet. Magma from the core had stopped flowing out into the basins of the oceans. And, the fountains of the deep had emptied themselves and were dry. Noah's God had pulled back his hand. The flood covered the whole earth to a depth twenty feet higher than the highest mountain of that time.

Deep below the surface of the water, the earth had been radically altered. Large land masses had been broken up. Where there had been plains, mountain ranges now stood. Where there had been rocky landscapes, now there were vast stretches of thick mud deposits brought in from far away by the flow of water. Thick layers of sea shells and calcium deposits that had been accumulating on the sea floor, were now spread out in layers where there had been tropical forests. And the billions of tons of trees and vegetation of a thousand forests, were now floating in immense rafts of debris waiting to be deposited somewhere when the waters subsided.

The family, unaware of these things below, went on with their routine, being careful to conserve on supplies. God had told Noah the rain would last forty days and nights, but the family had no idea how long they would be in the ark. There were a lot of mouths to feed. They just wanted to, sometime, somehow, somewhere, be back on land starting over.

As strange as the situation was, they would always have fond memories of those early days in the ark getting acquainted with a wonderful array of fascinating creatures who seemed grateful for the care and regular attention. But there were some long, difficult days ahead as they rode the floodwaters with not a trace of land in sight on the horizon.

Did you know? *When Mount St. Helens erupted in 1980, it laid down six hundred feet of sediment and gouged out a deep canyon in a matter of hours. Heat of the volcano melted the mountain's glacier which then, like a tsunami, swept an entire forest of millions of trees into a basin. Another eruption would bury this mat of debris and form a coal deposit. Catastrophic geologic change can happen very quickly. Water receding off the continent after a world-wide flood, could carve out the Grand Canyon in weeks or months.*

37

The Chores

From the first day, Anahit kept a record of days in the ark. Each morning she made a notch in the beam over the door to the living quarters. When the rain stopped there were forty-seven notches. She also worked with the other wives in keeping track of the stores. There were several food lockers throughout the ark. The family food storage room was stacked with crates, wine skins, oak barrels and clay jars.

At the top of the ark were three cisterns which collected rain-water for animal and human use. This is what Noah worried the most about. Would it rain again? How long would the water last? The flood water was brackish and muddy. So, if it didn't rain again, they would have to be careful with the water.

It took some time before they understood what to feed the animals. Some of the animals seemed to eat only certain plants and others, like the swine and rodents, ate anything. For the mammals they had baled large amounts of grasses and grains in tight bundles and stacked them in the lockers. For birds, reptiles and amphibians they had packed barrels-full of dried grasshoppers, crickets and worms. They had also barreled large quantities of nuts and seeds. All of this was because of the careful planning of Anahit.

After many days of trial and error, Ham figured out how to catch fish that schooled around the rafts of vegetation and these he fed to the bears, cats and sea birds. It was a long, learning experience, but they kept careful records and tried to improve on making sure each pair of animals had a daily supply of food and water.

And there was the waste.

Japheth devised a kind of hoe on a short stick which was used to scrape out cages into a trough in the passageway which was shoveled out each morning through two hatches in the rear. Every few days the crew would haul in buckets of flood water and wash down the decks. It wasn't long before everyone onboard, like farm families everywhere, got to actually like the smells of animals.

And, so far, the ark had remained upright and seaworthy.

"I'm actually a little amazed," Japheth told Noah. "The proportions that God gave us, the height, width and length of the ark, seem to be working. I mean, even in rough water, she has stayed upright and has always rolled to the right position."

"And," Noah added, "the amount of room we needed for the animals that came turned out to be right."

After more days drifting with no land in sight and little to do but feed, clean and make repairs, Shem proposed that they set up some kind of platform on the roof where they could get out of their tight quarters and get some fresh air. They all agreed and Japheth and Ham cut a hatch in the roof, installed a ladder, fastened four sturdy posts and strung hemp rope between them as a kind of guard rail. This gave them badly needed access, directly from their quarters, to a space on the roof. When the weather was agreeable, the upper deck became the favorite place to lounge between chores.

A rather monotonous string of days and weeks passed. Fortunately, it rained occasionally filling the cisterns. Wind storms came and went. The sky remained a dusty gray. The surface of the flood was nearly always agitated with strong currents, waves and an occasional series of mysteriously large swells. The family was disappointed to be unable to see the stars at night, for the stars had always been their companions. Stars had given them a sense of direction, signaled the change of seasons, signaled the beginning of festivals and been the subject of stories around the fire at night. But now, dust covered the heavens.

38

Story in the Stars

Then, one night, they were all reclining on the upper deck at the end of the day. Noah's wife had put out mats, a bowl of dried figs and some heads of grain, that they would rub between their hands, let the chaff drift away in the breeze and eat the kernels as they visited. They were talking about routine operations, the food levels, the repair of leaks, the health of the animals and how long they estimated they could continue with the supplies they had.

The sun had fallen below the horizon with the usual spectacular display of color. The night sky overhead slowly grew dark as it passed through its usual shades of gray.

"Look!" Ham cried out. "I see a star! What else could it be?"

They all looked to where he was pointing. Faintly, a single star could be seen half-way up from the horizon in a strangely black patch of sky. Then, as they looked, another and another star became visible. Three stars, neatly spaced. It was the belt of *Orion*, a star group well known to them all.

"Well, well," Noah said quietly. "He finally showed up. Maybe this is a sign of good things to come."

After more than a hundred days adrift, the gray haze was beginning to clear. It would be good to see the sun, moon and stars again.

"This is a time for celebration," Nayiri said and passed around the bowl of dried figs.

Slowly, the other stars of *Orion* could be seen, especially the very bright star above and to the left of the three famous stars of the belt.

"Remind us, father, of the meaning of this prince in the stars." Shem said.

"I cannot tell you the meaning, but you will not find a more glorious sign in the heavens," Noah said looking up. "He is always there, just beyond the region of the *Bull*. He is well known by all people, for he appears directly on the great circle around which all heavenly lights turn. His name from ancient times is *Orion*, which means *light*. Another ancient name given him is *Hahat*, which means *he who comes forth*. Another star in the group is *Heka,* which means *coming* and *Meissa*, which means *coming forth*. We have always known him to be the great warrior who comes in great light to save. Other stars in the group have important meanings. You can surely see *Betelgeuz*, in his right shoulder."

Noah pointed up and to the left of the three stars. They all knew that spectacular star.

"That is among the brightest and grandest of stars, which means *the coming of the branch*. You remember the branch in the hand of *Virgo,* the Virgin? She holds a branch in one hand, a star that means *seed* in the other and has a child in her lap. Who is she? And who is that child? Is he the seed

169

mentioned by our Creator? How can a virgin have a child?
And look at *Orion*'s feet."

They all looked intently, for the sky was now filled with
stars as sparkling bright as they'd ever seen.

"There is *Rigel,* which means *the foot that crushes.* And,
there is *Saiph* in his right thigh. It means *bruised.* You
remember, in the garden, when the Creator God spoke of the
seed of woman to the serpent, 'He shall crush your head and
you shall bruise his heel.' Well, that's the same word, *Saiph.*
He is wounded, bruised. See the star to the right on his belt?
That is *Al Nitak.* It means the *wounded one.*"

"Isn't he holding something, father?" Japheth asked.
There was no way to see these images of belts and branches
in the random assortment of stars. The message in the stars
was known only through specific star names and a very
precise legend passed down from Adam, learned from the
Creator himself. Other, myths and legends would be spun by
mankind, but the star names and the story Noah told, was
from the very beginning.

"Yes, two things, a lion's head in his left hand and a club
in his right," Noah answered. "And, he has a sword attached
to his belt, which for mysterious reasons has star names
meaning *lamb.* He is a conqueror. He is coming swiftly. He
is light. Yet, is come as a lamb and is wounded. I do not
understand how a conqueror can come as a lamb. But I do
understand the foot that crushes, for it is raised over the head
of the star group of the serpent. We all know who he is. But
who is this *Orion*? We don't know. All we know is there is
a great conflict between the champion of heaven, the seed of

170

a virgin and the enemy, an evil, cunning serpent. And we know who wins. That's all we know."

They sat and thought.

Then, Shem said, "There is another champion in the heavens, isn't there? *Ophiuchus*, the one who holds *Serpens*, the serpent and whose foot is on *Antares*, the red star, the heart of *Scorpio*. He also tells of the champion who comes."

"And what about the Bull?" Ham asked. "He has stars in his horns with names like *judgement* and *coming swiftly*. That seems to be part of a story that unfolds across the heavens. There certainly is a conflict. There is a figure who pours water, *Delu*, into the mouth of a fish, *Pisces*. There is a virgin and her seed. A champion coming in light. A lamb. A wounded one. A defeated serpent and scorpion. A lion killed. Judgement coming. My goodness! What does it all mean? There is a war going on and I have a feeling we are in the middle of it, somehow."

"And what about *Argo,*" Shem asked. "That's the great vessel in the stars. I think its stars mean *company of travelers*? Do you think that could be *us*?"

Noah looked directly at Shem for a long moment. He had never thought of that. Could *Argo* be us? It was a profound, shocking thought that sitting there on the roof of the ark, they could be playing a part in the celestial story.

From that evening on, the sky remained clear and the family spent many evenings observing the stars which rotated through the heavens telling a mysterious tale. What did all this mean? Fortunately, Noah and grandfather Lamech had passed on names of many stars and told many stories learned from Enoch and Methuselah. Though they didn't know the meaning, they had a strange sense of reassurance that there was, indeed, a champion over evil which would bring judgement to fulfill words spoken by the Creator at the beginning.

Did you know? *Names of the stars in all cultures and languages are pretty much the same. This would indicate that star names are extremely ancient. The Greeks spun their own fanciful story from the stars. But the names themselves, indicate a story very much parallel to the Bible's story of redemption. Orion is mentioned in the Book of Job, the most ancient of books. The Magi at Christ's birth knew exactly what the stars were saying. Why do we ignore them today?*

39

Landing on the Mountain

Anahit counted the notches on the door frame. One hundred and fifty days they had been in the ark, counting from when the rains first started. It had rained forty days and now there had been months of floating on a nearly featureless surface under a mostly gray sky. They had seen no sea birds or animals, except for a few flying fish and curious dolphins that had accompanied them as they drifted along. When they had drifted into large, thick mats of vegetation, they had seen swarms of insects, crabs and turtles clinging to the debris. But they had seen no island, no gray smudge of land on any distant horizon.

Anahit met Ham in the passageway.

"How are the food stores holding up?" she asked him.

"We've begun to cut back on grain for the large mammals. They've lost a few pounds but are doing well. In fact, we've added to our passenger list."

"How's that? Did you catch a dolphin and put him in the cistern?" Anahit joked.

"No. The small furry mammals seem to like to procreate. We have twice as many as when we started."

"Ha ha. That is a good thing, if we can get to land before the food runs out!"

As she said this a tremor shook the vessel, much like the earth quakes they felt in the compound. Ham and Anahit steadied themselves against the door frame and looked at each other. Did they hit a raft of large floating logs? What could that be?

Other family members came running past them toward the ladder going up to the upper deck.

"We must have hit something!" Shem yelled on his way up the ladder.

Looking over the side, they could see that the current was flowing past them creating a wake of turbulence that stretched off to the side. It could mean only one thing. They had struck bottom. Either there was a rock in the middle of the sea, or the water had begun to recede. The ark shifted and spun around for a few minutes. Then it released, causing everyone to nearly fall over on the deck. Then it caught again on what seemed more like sand or mud. And it stayed.

"Japheth!" Noah commanded. "Throw a line over the side with a cork and mark the water line. We need to know if the waters are receding and at what rate."

The atmosphere in the ark changed with this new development. Even the animals seemed to stir and become anxious. The motion of the ark had stopped and it took some time to get used to the feel of walking on a solid deck. And, there was some relief to the annoying sense of endless drifting. A new sense of hope put a bit of spring in everyone's step.

Unknown to anyone on board, there had been slow and steady movement of oceanic plates in the deep basins of the world's oceans. Far from the ark, in places seen only by deep diving creatures, the earth's crust had begun to shift as edges of continents crashed into each other driving mountain ranges up and sea basins down. The water that had been forced up onto land by plate movement and the influx of magma, now began to flow back over the rim of these immense basins and back into the deepening oceans of the planet. As in any flood, the water had reached its maximum height and was now flowing back. There would be catastrophic change to the surface of the earth as the water receded. Never in the long history of the earth has there been such a massive torrent of moving water. Each continent would drain, carrying along sediment as fine as clay and rocks as large as small mountains. Valleys and canyons would be gouged out in hours. Boulders a mile in diameter would be rolled along destroying everything in their path. The deposits laid down during the flood would drain off the continents into the surrounding seas leaving the continental shelves that would remain throughout history. Thick mats of vegetation would be covered over by mud slides and compressed forming future coal deposits. And, mass graves of creatures caught in the mud that accompanied the early phase of the flood, would be covered by sediment and fossilized.

The story written in the layers of rock and sediments and in the fossil record would inspire many fanciful interpretations. Many of them would have given Noah and his family a good laugh.

But to Noah and his family, drifting along in the ark, there was still just endless water with the new and positive sense that the end was not too far off. Enough water had drained into a distant basin to allow the ark to hit bottom on a mountain later to be called, Mount Ararat.

40

The Raven and Doves

It can take a long time for a drop of water to flow from a high place in the middle of a continent to a lower place where it finally enters the sea. So, the ark remained forty days in its place until the water gradually receded to where Noah could begin to see other small points of land in the distance. As the ark settled into its muddy place on the mountain, it rested at a slight angle making life even more difficult. Also, food stores were beginning to run low, so the family was desperate to get out of the ark onto level and dry land.

"Do you think the Creator God has forgotten us?" Shem asked his father. "The rain came, then the flood. Now we seem to be just caught between two worlds. We are here, stuck on a rock, without a land and without the means to live much longer in the ark."

To add to Shem's frustration, a very strong wind came suddenly up from the west forcing the two to leave the upper deck and take shelter below. Shem threw down his hat in anger.

But, Noah saw the wind as a good thing.

"Wind is going to speed up the drying process," he told the others. "It may be annoying, but we need all the help we can get getting rid of this water."

Japheth was eager to verify that his father was correct with his cork and line. He announced every inch of lower water levels. He took measurements over the side several times in a day and made a big point to prove to Shem that the water was dropping faster every day, especially since the wind had come up. Soon there was a stretch of shallow water around the ark, but waves still washed up against the side. It was unsafe to open the door. The crew continued with the chores, feeding and caring for the restless animal kingdom in their care. They couldn't fail now. Everything was at stake. All they needed was a reasonable expanse of dry, open land.

From the roof of the ark, they could see across what looked like a shallow sea spotted with small islands.

It was Shem's idea to release one of the birds.

"If we let a bird go and he doesn't return, wouldn't that mean he's found a place to live?" Shem asked Noah. "There may be livable land out there, just beyond what we can see."

Noah agreed. It was a good idea. But what bird? A seagull? No. It could survive in water. What about the raven? They knew the raven was a strong flier and a land bird. And, several pair had hatched during the voyage, so Shem brought one to Noah early the next morning. Noah released it through the netting by the upper deck. It circled over the ark looking a bit nervous about leaving its home, then caught the wind and disappeared into the distance. Then, around mid-day, Noah released a dove, which, like the raven, hung around the ark for a few minutes then flew down wind and was gone. They kept a look out for the two birds. Late in the afternoon the dove returned and was taken back into the ark, but the raven was never seen again. Had he found some way to survive out there until the water was dried up?

A week later, Noah released the dove again. This time it flew directly to a small, rocky island in the distance. Finding nothing of interest there, it flew off again and was soon out of sight. Several hours later it returned with a leaf in its mouth.

"That looks like an olive leaf to me," Shem said. "There is no way an olive plant could have leaves unless it had been growing in soil in the sunlight for a while. That means there's good dry land not too far over the horizon."

"Yeah, but how much of it?" Ham pressed.

With this meager intelligence, Noah waited another week, and brought the dove to the window again. This time, he held it in his hands before slipping her through the netting.

"Now I want you to go find us a place to live, little dove," he said looking her in the eye. "If you don't come back, that will mean you've found us a new land. Understood? Go. Prepare a place for us. Then, we and your mates, will come to join you there."

The dove turned her wise little eyes to the sky, then fluttered out through the opening and flew to the back of the ark and landed. She looked down the length of the long, wooden vessel and then out across the water. Her mate, she knew, was inside somewhere, still in his cage. She could see the man with the pale red cap still in the window watching her. This was the only home she knew, and wanted to stay, but there was the faint smell of something in the air that caught her attention. It stirred something up in her breast, a latent instinct to go and explore.

This time, she flew directly into the wind following the scent and an intuitive sense.

She looked back and could see the ark, now looking quite small in the distance resting on the muddy ledge of a large rocky island surrounded by water. Ahead, she could see more islands, and in the distance, on the horizon, a low gray silhouette. To the right and left there were more islands, but the scent she was following came from that long, gray place ahead. As she approached, she could see waves washing up on the rocky outcroppings of a substantial mainland. It had large, beaches of golden sand as far as she could see in either direction, and inland from the sand, there stood a row of trees stripped of their branches. And behind them was a massive field of low-growing green plants spread out before the foothills of a range of black mountains.

She pecked around in the sand where it met the fields and found deliciously fresh bugs. She explored a bush with small green leaves and buds that appeared to be new growth. All the greenery looked fresh and new. The landscape had been beat up as if by a great storm. There were no leaves or small branches on the large trees. Large rocks were strewn everywhere. But despite the obvious destruction, this was a place she knew she could call home. Everything she and her mates would need was here. It seemed like a good place to start a new life.

So, she stayed.

41

Opening the Door

Noah's ark continued to rest on a small patch of land, tilted against the muddy bank near the summit of Mount Ararat as the water of the earth drained slowly off into the expanding basins of the oceans.

"The waiting has got to come to an end," Anahit told Noah. "The food stores are nearly empty. We have to release some of the animals and let them graze for what they can get. There really is no option."

Noah could see the mountain under them was emerging rapidly from the water. The mud around the ark had cracked and dried. It looked to be safe to open the door and step out. Anahit was right. It was time.

"Ham, you can open the door," he said to his son. "Remove the wedges, swing it open, begin building a ramp with the timbers you have, and get ready to let the large mammals go."

It had been many months since Ham had driven those wedges in. He recalled how the door had sealed itself with just a few strokes of a mallet. Now, the day had come. He had become so accustomed to living in the confines of the ark, it was a strange thought to be able to go out the door and step onto dry ground.

He gathered the family by the door and began driving out the wedges. The seals released. Japheth and Shem attached lengths of hemp and lowered the door on its hinges making it into a temporary ramp. Noah, shielding his eyes with his forearm, stepped up to the opening and looked around. It was a bright landscape unlike any he had ever seen. They were in a field of rocks covered with a dry layer of brown mud and dead grasses of the sea. The terrain sloped down and away in all directions. It was plain that they had come to rest on the highest point in a vast, desolate land.

With help, Noah stepped down to the base of the door where it rested on the ground. He stood there for a moment and took it all in.

"God only knows how we will survive in a place like this," he said soberly to himself. "But we shall." And he stepped off into the new world.

Off in the distance there were other, lesser mountains and plateaus in all directions. When he looked closer at the soil around the ark, he could see sprouts of green everywhere among the rocks. Tufts of grass had begun and small bushes had leaves and buds. The air had the fresh smell of the land after a heavy mist had come. It did not look like a place of death. Rather, as Noah and the others looked around among the rocks, it began to look like a place ready to burst with life.

"What do you think?" his wife asked him as he stood there with his staff gazing out.

"Well, if you like new beginnings, then this is the land for you," he said looking out at the distant mountains.

"If you'll excuse us father," Ham interrupted, "We'd like to get started on the ramp."

"Go ahead," Noah said. "But we cannot release the animals quite yet."

Already, Ham and the others had slid some beams up to the doorway and were planning the ramp. They were very anxious to get it constructed. The tilt of the ark toward the door made the task much easier. It was only about ten feet to the ground.

It did not take long for the brothers, anxious to begin the unloading process, to build the ramp. But Noah did not give permission to let animals out. He said he was waiting for the right time. Anahit was becoming very concerned. She asked the others to speak to him. The animals stirred in their stalls. Tension grew. Food for some animals had run out. But Noah held firm.

"I'm sorry. But it is not time," is all he would say.

Nearly a month after the door had been opened, when Noah was just over six-hundred and one years old, the moment came. In his quiet time on the beam he had a very clear word from the Lord in his spirit. It was time to begin letting the animals out.

42

The New Land

As the netting was removed, birds emerged from the windows along both sides of the ark. They circled around aimlessly and rested back on the roof. Little by little they ventured out across the landscape landing on rocks and bushes, pecking at the ground and looking quite pleased.

The first pair of four-legged animals to poke their heads out and wander down the ramp was a pair of furry, gray koala bears with a little one clinging to his mother's back. They waddled down the ramp, looked around and stood there blinking as others came rushing past. Then came the kangaroo, the canines, the bears and deer. Small animals scurried under the legs of the others. Some hid under the ramp. Everyone stood back when the elephants and rhinos came down.

It was a delightful, even humorous sight.

The more shy creatures slipped out of sight under the ark into the shade. Long-legged storks strutted down the ramp and began testing their great wings frightening the rabbits and squirrels. Noah and Nayiri stood off to the side watching the spectacle as the sons and their wives were inside opening cages and guiding a continuous line of critters down the passageways and out the door. Some refused to move and were left to make the decision to leave in their own time.

Anahit went up to the top deck to watch. Animals that were not hiding under the ark had spread out around the vessel gathering in small groups according to similar kinds. Animals of prey naturally kept as far away from the predators as they could. No serious fights broke out or threats made. She watched Ham as he went around with a stick dispersing the herd around the ark, encouraging them to range further out to find sustenance among the rocks and sparce foliage in the area. Birds were picking in the soil. Squirrels were digging. Deer were chewing on branches. The elephants were poking their trunks around in the dry mats of sea grasses. The big cats had wandered a long way off together and were reclining in the shade of a large rock.

Anahit had worried about this moment. Being a lover of animals, she was aware of the possibility that some may be lost. How would they get along? Would the rabbits survive? Just watching, she could see that the animals were effectively using their natural defenses. The predators seemed to be instinctively tempering their aggressiveness, at least for the time being. And, the small animals, used to being chased, had already scampered off and were beginning to disappear in the distance.

She could see that the flood had left edible things behind, because the ground around the ark was soon dug up and turned over as the hungry animals searched for and found their first fresh meals. By late afternoon, nearly all the animals had left the area. Only a few pairs of domesticated animals and birds remained, kept in pens and cages temporarily set up near the ark. The ground around the ark was a dug-up mess of fur, feathers and animal droppings.

That evening, the family sat around an oil lamp in the living quarters of a very quiet ark sharing stories and discussing plans for the future. There were only the quiet stirrings of a pair of kangaroos in an adjacent stall, caught in the process of giving birth. And, there was the whirring of two ruby-throated humming birds sipping from a small jar of honey water that Anahit had set out for them.

"What do you think, family? Did we succeed at the job given to us?" Noah asked the group.

"Well," Ham answered, "We just released more animals than we took onboard. That is success."

Then putting his arm around his beloved wife and drawing her toward him, he said, "And I intend to do my part, to be fruitful and to multiply. To me, that will be success!"

They all laughed. They were enjoying the moment, the sense of having overcome the impossible.

43

What Lies Ahead

Shem rose early the next morning to check on the temporary animal pens they had set up for sheep and cattle, the animals Noah called "clean" animals. In the morning light he was pleased to see that bits of vegetation had already begun to give the brown landscape a greenish tint. Grasses were coming up everywhere and the bushes no longer were bare and lifeless. A single body of water could be seen in a low area several miles down the side of the mountain. The flood had surely retreated. Looking across the valley to the west, he could see a very promising land that stretched from north to south. Could that land be their their new home?

As he was looking out across the vista, he noticed his father's pale red cap moving along the edge of a field behind the ark. Shem had to laugh. Ha. Already, he's out there, scouting out a place to sit and think and talk to his Creator God! That is where this whole story began. And now, the next chapter of our lives, Shem thought, will be determined by what he hears next on his bench down there in the rocks.

He was proud to be the son of such a peculiar man! When all others put their confidence in Man's ability to determine his own destiny, an ability proven inadequate at best, his father trusted in what seemed more lasting and transcendent. Old Noah really was unique in all the world, among all the men that Shem had known. And, in that moment, Shem determined in his heart to follow in his father's ways.

Some time later, Noah called everyone together.

"Ham, could you and Shem take two of the cattle, good clean ones, and follow me? And, Anahit, could you please take two birds from the pen and come too? We are going to make an offering to the Lord. And my dear," he said to Nayiri, "could you please bring a sharp knife. I have pitch and a fire tool."

"An offering?" Japheth protested. "We have so little to spare!"

Noah turned and began walking down the mountainside as if he hadn't heard Japheth. He headed toward the place Shem had seen him and, as he walked, he gathered up dead sticks and brush. In a few minutes the brothers and their wives came along behind with the two sheep and two birds.

Noah may have been hard of hearing at his age, or he was too far ahead to hear the murmurings, but there was quite a bit of complaining among the family members as they followed.

They came, finally, to a large flat ledge on the mountainside, where Noah had piled a number of rocks into a kind of altar. It was as high as a man's chest and as broad as a man is tall. Noah had already heaped dry wooden fuel onto the altar. He asked them to prepare the sacrifices.

This was not new to them. In their tradition, at special occasions, offerings were given as a form of worship. They knew all about what happened in the garden of Eden. They knew Able had brought the best of his flock to the altar and Cain had brought what was convenient from the field. They knew whose sacrifice had been accepted. Their murmurings ended as they soberly prepared the offerings and laid them on the altar. Then they turned and stood with long faces before Noah.

Noah was smiling. He stood in his yellow tunic and pale red cap with a broad smile on his face! To everyone's surprise he clapped his hands in joy, then spread out his arms and tried to gather them all in an embrace. Tears rolled down his face. He could hardly speak.

"My dear, troubled family!" he cried. "Be thankful! Look what God has done! He has chosen us, to begin again through us! I am so thankful to him for carrying us through! For carrying us safely above the floodwaters of his judgement. And, I am so thankful for you! I am grateful for your willingness to follow his commands, to build the ark and to put your faith in his words. You put your faith in *me.* Yes. But, ultimately, it was faith in *him.* We did all according to *his* word. And what *he* said came to pass."

He lit the fire and they all waited there near the altar until the entire offering was consumed. Smoke rose and drifted across the valley toward the distant land on the horizon. The family sat on the rocks, meditated on what Noah had said and talked amongst themselves about the future and about what they might find on that distant land to the west.

Japheth said what was on all their minds.

"Father, we don't know how to feel about all that has happened. Didn't we just experience a hundred years of toil and persecution? Wasn't the flood a terrible tragedy? How can we be worshipping, making offerings at a time like this?"

"Yes." Noah answered. "Those years leading up to the flood were awful. It would have been easy to fall into despair. And the flood itself was a devastating thing. It would be easy to despair now. But sometimes what looks like the agony of death and a time to despair, is actually the pain of new birth and a time to rejoice. I choose to see these difficult times as good, just and a new beginning."

Then Noah made a large sweeping gesture with his arm out toward the west.

"Look! That land is our future. It is up to us to decide how we will live, who we will serve. Our choice will determine what kind of world we build."

The family stood together there by the smoking altar looking out across the valley. Rain clouds drifted across the scene from the north and they could see gray streaks of rain falling onto the land in the distance. They had been through so much and were worn down and tired. The family just wanted to put the floodwaters, the ark, the past, everything, behind them and move on to a new life.

"Hey look!" Ham exclaimed loudly, pointing out across the valley. "What is that?"

They had gotten used to seeing strange clouds since the beginning of the flood, but, now, as they looked, something unique was in the sky. A bow of many colors was beginning to appear from horizon to horizon. It was perfectly shaped and other-worldly. They stood watching, speechless. As the bow formed and became more vivid, a second, fainter bow formed below the first. The vision was distant, yet near. It hung in space and glowed like a string of brilliant jewels in a mist. Then, as mysteriously as it appeared, it began to fade.

Noah and the three sons took off their caps and knelt. The wives huddled together by the altar. No one knew what to say.

Then, they heard the Creator God speak. None of them would be able to describe later what the voice sounded like. But they all heard it and would remember every word.

"I make a promise to you," the voice said, "and to your descendants and all living creatures."

The Creator promised to never again destroy life on earth with a flood. The rainbow in the clouds would always be a sign, he told them, of this promise between him and all life on the earth. He would remember it. And they were also to remember it, whenever they saw a rainbow.

Several moments passed. Noah was the first to move. The others were silent and dumbfounded by what they had just witnessed. Noah motioned them all to come to him. They stood there with wide eyes looking back and forth between the fading rainbow and Noah, who was grinning mischievously.

"My dear family, you've often asked me," he said with a wink, "what it's like to hear God's voice. Well, now you know."

Acknowledgements

I am especially indebted to the writings of Dr. John D. Morris, geologist, professor, creation scientist, and author. His book, *The Global Flood, Unlocking Earth's Geologic History*, 2012, copyrighted by the Institute for Creation Research, provided the scientific and theoretical basis for my understanding of geologic causes and effects of the flood in my story of Noah.

The theological writings of A.W. Tozer, regarding the attributes of God, God's pursuit of Man and the spiritual state of mankind, helped me understand Noah's dependence upon the character of God and Man's unfortunate dependence upon himself.

I am thankful for the writings of J. Vernon McGee, especially Volume 1 of his *Thru The Bible* series, for theological insight into the first nine chapters of Genesis and his very helpful genealogical chart.

Made in the USA
Monee, IL
12 March 2022